SINEMA 3:

THE TROY CONSORTIUM

Rod Glenn

www.rodglenn.com

A Wild Wolf Publication

Published by Wild Wolf Publishing in 2013

Copyright © 2013 Rod Glenn

ISBN: 978-1-907954-31-3
Also available as an e-book

www.wildwolfpublishing.com

FURTHER WORKS BY ROD GLENN

The King of America (2006)
Sinema: The Northumberland Massacre (2007)
The King of America: Epic Edition (2008)
Radgepacket: Tales from the Inner City (2008, contributor)
The Killing Moon (2009)
Sinema 2: Sympathy for the Devil (2011)
Holiday of the Dead (2011, contributor)
Wild Wolf's Twisted Tails (2013, contributor)
Action: Pulse Pounding Tales Volume 2 (2013, contributor)

PRAISE FOR SINEMA

"One the most heart racing, jaw-dropping novels that I have ever dared to finish."
~ The Crack Magazine

"A truly chilling novel."
~ Borders Books

"An exploration of pure evil."
~ Remotegoat.co.uk

"Compelling and disturbing."
~ Melrose Books

"Sinema is unnerving, disturbing and chilling. It will delight fans of horror and thrillers alike."
~ Holly A Harvey, award-winning author

"Darkly imaginative."
~ Discovered Authors

Thank you to my gorgeous wife for putting up with my weird ways and for not listening to her friends when they tell her that she needs to worry about me!

Unleash Hell ...

FOREWORD

Okay, I know, I know, I said *Sympathy for the Devil* would be the last *Sinema* novel, but what can I say? Han Whitman just would not die, for God's sake. I tried, I really did! I shot him, stabbed him and tortured the living shit out of him (pardon my French). What could I do?

It's probably some sort of aversion to suicide, I guess, given that Han Whitman is more me than I am, if that makes any sense whatsoever. And, no, I haven't started killing people … yet.

Mere days after the final proof of *Sympathy for the Devil* had been accepted for publication, my mind began to click and whir with previously unseen possibilities of where to take the story next.

As my wife will profess, my mind works in dark and mysterious ways …

So, here we are, *The Troy Consortium*. Sorry!

If you go chasing rabbits …

PROLOGUE

HAYDON MASS MURDERER GUNNED DOWN!

NORTHUMBERLAND MASSACRE KILLER DEAD!

NOTORIOUS SERIAL KILLER, HANNIBAL WHITMAN, SHOT DEAD!

#hanwhitman

#northumberlandmassacre

#haydonmassacre

Menacing storm clouds filled the sky. The sea off the Dorset coast mirrored it, a dark and tumultuous tempest.

The young female reporter shivered and gulped in a breath. The wind was building, forcing her to swipe blonde locks out of her face, before saying to the cameraman, "Are we fucking ready yet, Liam?"

"Nearly," the cameraman said, "they're bumping us up to headline."

"The biggest fucking story this century is exploding across the entire planet and I'm standing here freezing my tits off."

"Butter wouldn't melt, eh, Dawn?" he replied, shaking his head.

"Fuck you. This is the big one."

With an exasperated sigh, the cameraman said, "Okay, here we go, live in five, four ..."

The reporter angrily swept the hair from her face one more time then, in her best solemn, yet captivating tone, she spoke into the camera. "At ten-thirty AM this morning, a police spokesperson confirmed that the fugitive known as Hannibal Whitman, the suspect in the notorious Haydon massacre two and a half years ago, has been shot dead in a standoff with armed police officers near Weymouth in Dorset. Details are vague at the moment, but it is believed that he was cornered after the slaughter on the prison ship *The Weare* late last night ..."

***

A face loomed in close, wide mouth sneering, black eyes glaring. It was a man's face, but contorted beyond belief into an enraged beast.

"I will stick my fucking hands into that open hole in the side of what's left of your face and peel the whole fucker right off!" the man-creature shrieked, close enough for hot spittle to spray his burning face.

Suddenly, there was a thunderous crash, like being trapped in an oil drum that's been thrown off the edge of a cliff.

Faces above him, speaking soundlessly. A feeling of moving, but staying still.

"Nobody understands!" the man-creature spat. "This ... monster can't be tried. The system can't cope with someone like him. He has to die and he has to suffer to his very last breath ... which will be very soon."

14

Another deafening roar.

"Are you in some kind of trouble?" A woman this time, fearful, desperate. Pale blue eyes imploring.

"Run, mate! It's a fucking trap!" Mr Brown screams, blood bubbling on his crimson lips.

A high-pitched squeal, like the death rattle of a dolphin.

"We'll know why, just you and I, know true love ways ..."

Searing heat, crisping and bubbling flesh ...

A trembling, frail woman, like a wounded rabbit, aiming a gun. A flash of light ...

I want to play a game.

(HAPTER 1

A gentle breeze caressed his face. The man's eyes flickered open. His vision was as blurred as his thoughts. Where was he? What happened? Unanswered questions filled his mind. Confusion spiked with fear.

As his eyesight gradually returned to him, he realised that his limbs were restricted. Craning his neck, he realised that he was laid flat out on the ground in just his white sirwal pants. His arms and legs were drawn tight and strapped to four spikes that had been driven deep into the compacted dirt. The cold ground sent a shiver through his body.

The morning sun was just peeking above the quarry walls. The quarry itself appeared deserted, save for derelict machinery and a couple of portacabins.

One particular piece of machinery was sat a few feet away from his tethered feet. The hulking tractor-mounted road roller was silent and unmoving, but no less intimidating.

His throat felt parched, but he shouted out, "Hello! Is there anyone there? Sasha?" He waited, listening. Silence, except for the breeze. "Help!"

A shadow played across his face. A man in a flowing black long coat appeared above him. He was as tall as he was broad, with dark, piercing features and a trim goatee beard. He had bright, intelligent eyes and an almost contemplative look.

There was an instant flicker of relief on the prone man's face, but it vanished on seeing the big man produce a silver dagger with an ornate red cross on its hilt.

"Who—"

The big man cut him off with a wave of the dagger, the blade glinting in the morning sunshine. "Be silent," he said, his voice a deep baritone. "My name is Lionheart and you are my prisoner."

"What? Prisoner? Why?"

With a sigh, the man said, "I will cut you and let you die a very slow death if you speak without permission one more time. Is that understood?"

The man opened his mouth to speak, but then quickly closed it and nodded instead.

"Good," Lionheart said and smiled. "Now, to business. You have been secured in front of this … I suppose the old-fashioned term is steamroller, although this particular one is of course not steam-powered."

He allowed the man the time to study the giant metal beast at his feet before his gaze returned to his captor. He could see the fear rising in the man; the beads of sweat, the trembling in his limbs, the bobbing up and down of his Adam's apple, his wide, darting eyes. It was exquisite. He allowed himself a moment to savour it.

"I can see that you are beginning to appreciate the gravity of your situation. You do, however, have a choice, which is more merciful than your brethren have been."

The man opened his mouth again, but quickly clamped it shut. Instead, he shook his head furiously.

"By your brethren, I mean the marauding infidels raping our lands and corrupting our gene pool. Our bleeding heart liberals welcome you in with open arms and in return, you plot and scheme our destruction. You have been tried and found guilty."

Lionheart's attention was drawn to something beyond the tethered man. Glancing back at the man, he continued, "As I said, you have been blessed with a choice. The crane behind you has a woman suspended from it."

17

The man arched his neck. A woman was indeed dangling from a grapple over one hundred feet above the unyielding ground. He recognised the flapping white bed gown, her flowing black hair and even the slender curves of her feet. "Sasha!" he screamed, twisting and wrenching at his bonds. "No, please!"

Lionheart's eyes lingered on the suspended woman, watching as her gown fluttered, revealing her thighs and a glimpse of black pubic hair. He licked his lips then turned his attention back to the Saracen. "Your attention, if you please, Mika. I will allow you that outburst. However, listen very carefully. Your choice is this: save yourself or save your wife. Now, feel free to speak."

"Why are you doing this? I am a Muslim, but I do not preach hatred. This is my country, my home!"

"Spare me your Saracen lies. You will die or your whore will die in your stead." Lionheart bent down and placed a remote control in Mika's hand. "If you press the button on that remote control in less than five minutes, the steamroller will slowly make its way to your wife. It will stop with its trailer beneath her and she will fall into the safety of the hay inside it." He paused for dramatic effect and then added, "As you are in its path, the steamroller will, of course, crush you in the process."

Mika was shaking his head and opened his mouth to speak. Lionheart cut him off and said, "If you do not push the button, your miserable life will be spared, but your wife will plummet to the ground. The impact will smash almost every bone in her delicate body and, if she miraculously survives the initial impact, she will die of shock or blood loss long before you are freed to save her."

"Please don't do this! We haven't harmed anyone!"

Lionheart glanced at his watch. "You have less than three minutes to decide."

Mika strained his neck and screamed out once more, "Sasha!"

"Mika!" she screamed back at him. "Help me!" She had clearly only just woken up and was now frantically kicking her legs in blind panic. She kept screaming.

He turned back to Lionheart. "Why are you doing this? You monster!"

"I am not a monster. I am merely a faithful soldier. I did not start this war, but I will do everything in my power to win it." He checked his watch one more time. "You have sixty seconds left to make your choice."

Mika stared from his hysterical wife to the small object in his hand. It had a single red button. If he pressed it, he died, but his wife would be saved. But would she? And would he if he didn't press it? Were they both destined to die regardless?

"How do I know you won't just kill us both anyway?" he blurted out, his thumb trembling over the button.

Lionheart pocketed the dagger and folded his arms. "You have my word." As he turned and strode away, he said, "Goodbye."

His heart hammered in his chest and his breaths became shallow pants. His eyes stared wildly at the man strolling away. His wavering lips uttered, "Sasha ..." He pressed the button.

The engine in the tractor growled into life and the cumbersome machine began to edge forward, the roller turning and grinding small rocks into the ground.

As it drew nearer, he muttered a prayer then shouted, "Sasha, I love you!"

The giant roller struck his bare feet, curling his toes and then, with a series of pops and cracks, it crushed them under its steady advance. Mika screamed as blood squirted out onto the sandy dirt. The roller continued over his shins and up his legs, squashing flesh and splintering bones. By the time it reached his knees, the blinding agony became too much. He fell unconscious and was dead by the time it crushed his pelvis.

Sasha watched, sobbing and screaming as the machine crushed her husband inch by slow inch. It reached his head last, popping it as easily as a water balloon. It trundled on, oblivious. All it left was a pulped smear in its wake.

As the tractor slowly pulled up beneath her, there was an audible click and the grapple pincers parted.

A screech caught on her terrified lips as she fell. The tractor was still moving as she struck the roof. The protruding exhaust tore her arm from its socket as her back and legs smashed against metal.

She lay twitching, blood cascading down from the roof over the windscreen.

Lionheart stopped and looked around. Clicking his tongue, he glanced at his watch and said, "You took too long to decide." As he continued to his car, he added as an afterthought, "A pity, but she had lain with the enemy, so a just outcome."

It's Alive!

CHAPTER 2

With lids like slabs of concrete, Han Whitman gradually opened his eyes to an impossibly bright room. The air was cool and silent, apart from the rhythmic beeping of monitoring equipment.

The room suddenly pitched and spun and Han lurched up, overwhelmed with nausea. A firm pair of hands appeared and pressed him back down onto the bed. "Don't move," the stern woman's voice commanded.

Glancing to his side, he saw that the voice belonged to a nurse who was built like a Russian shot putter. Despite her formidable build, she had a genuinely concerned expression.

Licking his dry lips, Han managed, "What … Where am I?" His throat felt like two sheets of sandpaper rubbing together.

The nurse glanced over her shoulder.

A second voice, male this time, said, "Leave us, please."

The nurse nodded and left the room without another word. Han craned his neck to see the owner of the new voice.

A man was sitting in the corner of the room. He was dressed in a drab grey business suit, with a raincoat draped over his lap. He appeared to be in his mid thirties, average height, average weight, short brown hair. Mr Average. His expression was difficult to read, but then he offered a thin smile. In a friendly tone, he said, "Mr Whitman, my name's Gabriel."

Han stared at him for a time, his eyesight still blurred around the edges, trying to make sense of his situation. He coughed then said, "I wasn't quite expecting Heaven ... not with my reputation."

Gabriel's smile broadened. "You're not dead, Mr Whitman."

After drawing a shaky breath, Han said, "Well ... in that case, nice to meet you. I think." After a moment's thought, he added, "Mr Whitman is ... my ..." He struggled for the right words.

"Mr Whitman," the man continued unperturbed, "you had us quite concerned there for a while. I thought all of our efforts might have gone to waste."

"Where am I?" He coughed again and tried to swallow. "Who ..." His voice gave out.

An image of Will Wright screaming, with drill in hand and blood splattered across his chest, danced across his vision. Then Carol Belmont, crying, revolver in trembling hand, pleading with him.

His mind was a jumble of images, mixed up and out of order. *Carol didn't shoot Will, just me ... Who shot Will? Charlie? No, Charlie shot Perry. The police shot Will. Very kind of them.*

Gabriel stood up, throwing his coat over the chair. He walked over to the bed and filled a beaker with water from a jug that was set on the cabinet beside the bed. "You've been out for quite a while. Here, drink some water." He held the beaker close to Han's chin so that he could take the drinking straw into his mouth. The cool water slipped down his parched throat. He felt like John Mills taking that first sip of ice-cold beer in Alex.

"Worth waiting for," Han said as the man set the beaker back down.

"You're welcome," Gabriel replied. "To answer your questions, I work for an organisation called the Troy Consortium."

The name instantly struck a chord. "My dad ... he mentioned something about that." Visions of his father swam in front of his eyes. His condescendence, his pity then the anger and disgust. Staring down at him ... *There's so much more to tell you – the Troy Consortium ... our future together ...*

He shook his head to dispel them.

"Yes, your father did work for us, although I feel obliged to say that even if you hadn't have killed him we were going to terminate his contract. He went somewhat off reservation, I'm disappointed to say."

"Off reservation? He murdered my mum and my best friend. What sort of people do you hire round here?" He left his next obvious question unasked.

"Your father, like our other operatives have to work within a strict remit – that is part of the deal for their continued existence. Your father was tasked to eliminate certain undesirables and, later on, to recruit you. He was supposed to feed targets to you and build up a bond, but he stepped over the line. Way over the line."

"You guys *hire* psychopathic killers?"

"Serial killers, to be precise, although not exclusively. We capture them then give them an ultimatum – work for us under our supervision to our exact guidelines or … be terminated. That is precisely the deal I am about to offer you."

His brain must have been misfiring in some quite spectacular ways to dream this one up. Han couldn't believe what he was hearing. This had to be some sort of dream. It was a fucking dodgy film plot!

Or no, maybe not a dream. He had to be dead, regardless of what the fallen angel was saying. Carol Belmont had killed him and this was his Hell. Bit of a strange Hell, but at least there didn't appear to be any red hot pokers. Yet.

Gabriel continued, "We had our own trauma team standing by and whisked you off to a private facility where we had some of the best surgeons in Britain waiting to operate. Even with our world class facilities it was still touch and go. As well as the near fatal gunshot wound, you have undergone extensive facial and knee reconstructive surgery, not to mention the other less life-threatening injuries. We have put you back together pretty well, but it has taken three months where they have had to keep you in a medically induced coma." With a nod towards Han's hand, he added, "The only things they weren't able to fix were your two fingers – we

23

couldn't locate them in time. But I think you can consider that a very minor detail considering."

Han lifted his right hand. The little finger and ring finger were both gone; less than an inch stub remained of each. They had already healed well.

His hand then moved to his face. He hesitated at first, but then tentatively, he extended his remaining fingers and touched bandages. "My face?"

"You have undergone four operations on your face alone," Gabriel said. "While they were reconstructing the damaged area they also made some minor alterations to your nose, cheekbones and chin. It's standard procedure to alter the physical appearance of a potential new candidate."

Han stared at him. "I don't look like me anymore?"

"I haven't seen the final results, but I'm told you'll look similar, but with some marked facial differences. If you're going to join the team, it's an absolute must, I'm afraid." His tone was genuinely apologetic. With a smile, he added, "So, what do you say?"

Han snorted and the action seemed to make several parts of his body ache. Groaning, he said, "What do I say? I don't think I've got much choice here, do I?"

Gabriel shook his head. "On the contrary, there's always a choice. You can work with us or it's a simple and painless lethal injection."

"Well, let me see, I must weigh up all the options ..."

Gabriel laughed. "I'm going to like working with you, Han. I'm going to be your handler."

"How many other *operatives* do you have?"

"Not including you, there are currently three active serial killers in the UK. We manage two of them and are actively recruiting the third. We have other types of operatives as well, but you chaps are our star assets."

"So, as long as they're killing who you want them to kill you allow them to get on with it?"

Gabriel nodded. "Within our guidelines, but, in a nutshell, yes. You will be under strict supervision at all times, of course. We don't want another incident like your father."

"Heaven forbid," Han muttered.

Gabriel stared at him for a time then said, "The Troy Consortium was established to ensure that Great Britain remained strong on the inside as well as outwardly. For decades, certain social, criminal, political and religious elements have sought to rape or destabilise our good nation. Many work beyond the reaches of the law or manage to worm their way through an inadequate system, leaving the police and judicial systems unable to respond. That is where we step in. We are on the frontline in the battle to maintain order in a world that is becoming more unstable and chaotic with each passing year. I don't expect you to agree with our ideals, but I do expect you to abide by them. There are no second chances. This is your one chance." Gabriel's tone turned solemn. "Step out of line once and your contract will be terminated."

Han managed a stiff nod.

Gabriel stood up and smoothed an imaginary crease in his suit jacket before saying, "Right, I had better leave you to it. You've still got a long way to go before you'll be back to your best. Once you're ready we'll then start your training and discuss your role in more detail. Get plenty of rest."

Gabriel picked up his coat on the way out and then left Han alone. He stared at the closed door for some time, his mind a torrent of thoughts and memories.

He had been plucked from the jaws of death by some clandestine outfit who were trying to make Britain a better place. And how were they doing it? Using lunatic serial killers, present company included. His life had gone from video shop owner, to mass murderer, to vigilante and now to some bloody Jason Bourne-type madness. It just seemed absurd. And yet, at the same time, it was in keeping with Phase Two of his experiment. His father knew about the experiment, so surely Gabriel and the Troy Consortium must too. Given that, they would think that Han of all people was perfect for the job, taking only the Phase Two part into account, of course.

There was not a lot he could do other than play along and see how it panned out. He was a serial killer, not a company spook. He worked alone without rules or restrictions, that was part of the ethos. This wasn't his cup of tea, but he had to be smart and patient. On the plus side, Gabriel seemed like a genial enough bloke. And they had saved his life. Maybe it could be fun.

"Come up to the lab and see what's on the slab," he muttered to himself with a snort.

Han fell silent. The soft beeping continued in time with his beating heart. He placed his hand on his chest and felt the gentle rise and fall. His heart was beating. He was alive and the Troy Consortium was real.

Han let his three-fingered hand fall down by his side and he stared at the bare clinical walls around him. His thoughts turned to Cara. What must she be going through? What would she have been told about him? He could only imagine the feeding frenzy the press would have had – editors and reporters all around the country must have been jacking off all and sundry to get the inside scoop. She would have been hounded beyond belief. Would she be wrestling between horror and grief? Or would the grief have been consumed by the horror? She had loved him. She had told him, but deep down he had known it without having to hear the words. And he had loved her … still loved her. Could she possibly feel anything for him now? Anything, other than disgust?

His mutilated hand returned to his bandaged face once more and covered his eyes.

It's the highest form of public service.

CHAPTER 3

A single overhead strip light flickered intermittently, casting dancing shadows across the grubby walls and floor of the lockup garage.

Han's breath hung in the dank air in front of him. Other smells lingered just beneath the damp; unpleasant smells. Sweet decay.

Han's footsteps echoed on wet concrete as he stepped into the middle of the room. The workbench was there, where he remembered it. A fetid old blanket had been thrown over it, but there was something underneath. He could make out the distinct contours of a person. Dark glistening stains were spreading from the person's head, torso and legs.

This can't be, Han thought, shaking his head vehemently. I made it. I'm alive.

His outstretched hand trembled as it tentatively gripped the edge of the stinking shroud. His Adam's apple bobbed uncontrollably as he gathered his nerve. Slowly, he drew the blanket down from the person's head. Matted short ginger hair, receding hairline ... Han paused, his hand trembling so much that his right had to stabilise it. He noticed that two fingers were missing. Well done, Tony ... Tony? No, that's not right. Right?

He shook his head and the whole room shuddered like a bad acid trip.

Steadying himself against the bench, he told himself to man up then grabbed the blanket once more. With one sharp tug, it fell away from the face. The left cheek was gone, revealing blackened teeth bordering a gaping void. The

27

stench of barbequed flesh stung his nostrils and he jerked back, gagging. Something caught his attention from the still smouldering hole. Movement. Leaning closer, Han squinted in an effort to pierce the darkness.

Suddenly a bloated cockroach emerged, antennae probing the air, scrawny hairy limbs skittering over crisp flesh.

Han recoiled in horror, staggering into a second workbench. Turning, his eyes fell upon a rusted collection of tools; garden shears, blow torch, drill, Stanley knife, screwdrivers, hammers. They were all dripping with blood and gore. Gasping for breath, Han stumbled blindly away. Head swimming, he blundered into the wall. The slimy cold surface pressed against his clammy skin. He opened his eyes and caught his reflection in a wall-mounted mirror. The glass was smeared, but he recognised himself in the stranger that stared back at him. The shakes faded and the hyperventilating subsided, leaving a profound sense of serenity.

A smile played across his lips.

Han is dead. Long live Han.

***

The next month saw Han undergo intensive physiotherapy. It took some work just to get walking properly again on his state-of-the-art equivalent to a pensioner's knee replacement. His drilled foot did not make things any easier. The constant pain throughout, what felt like his entire body, alternated between dull aches and acute spikes, depending upon the activity. He was extremely weak at first, but his two fanatical physioterrorists were utterly relentless. They had a schedule to stick to and no one was going to fuck with that.

As well as the physical rehabilitation, he was also being pumped full of a concoction of drugs and vitamins to speed up the recovery process and re-build muscle mass.

Two weeks into his therapy, Han was finally able to get a look at his new face.

The nurse stepped back, holding the bandages in her hands. Han was half expecting a look of horror. *Herr doktor, we've created a monster!* Cue lung-rupturing scream. Instead, she just stared with professional indifference.

"Can you give me a moment?"

The nurse nodded and left the room without a word.

It was with marked trepidation that Han slowly held the mirror up to his newly unveiled face. His fears of having been transformed into some grotesque Herbert West creation/Elephant Man hybrid proved unfounded.

With a trembling sigh of relief, he studied his new reflection. He was still himself, just a bit ... different. Everything looked a little more pronounced – a bigger nose, more prominent chin and cheekbones. His left cheek was discoloured and more sunken in comparison to the right. The surgeons had built it up over the months with skin and tissue grafts, but it still had some healing to do.

They told him that there was still some swelling and that over time his cheek would fill out more and the skin tone would gradually improve to a point where it would resemble more of a birthmark.

Was this Han's real face finally revealed, as opposed to the proverbial mask that he used to wear in his previous life? Maybe. He didn't look too bad at all, given the injuries that he had sustained at Will's hands, but he did look ... weird ... different.

The first few days of catching a glimpse of his reflection in the mirror induced double takes that would sometimes leave his heart hammering in his chest. The initial shock would then give way to a feeling of elation.

His dreams were dominated by transformation. Not in a disturbing way, like Lisa transforming into a John Landis creation, but in a refreshingly optimistic one.

For a time, he really wasn't sure who he was anymore, some days feeling reborn as the real Han Whitman then other days maudlin over his past life with Cara, Perry and his family. But with the passage of time came stability. Instead of dwelling on it, he embraced it. Out with the old and in with the new.

Gabriel visited often as his strength steadily improved. He kept their conversations casual, asking about his progress, how he was feeling, rather than discussing any further details about the Troy Consortium. Han let it go, biding his time, building up his strength.

As his physiotherapy regime changed from recovery to more strength and fitness, he was moved to a new facility. With this being the Troy Consortium, a simple transfer was out of the question.

After being sat in a wheel chair, he was blindfolded and ears plugged and then fresh bandages were wrapped around his head, concealing the blindfold and plugs. They were not taking any chances. He was not going to be allowed to see or hear anything of where he had been or where he was going. Whether it was just for his benefit or also for casual observers was unclear, but it was probably both.

After being wheeled down a couple of corridors and through a few sets of doors, he suddenly felt a cold breeze on the exposed lower half of his face. He stole a moment to fill his lungs with cold sweet-smelling air, tinged with the faint aroma of nearby woodland. He strained to hear the muffled sounds of rustling leaves amidst footsteps and then an engine gunned, drowning everything else out.

He was pushed up a ramp and then a door closed behind him. He smelled the clean, disinfected interior of what was probably some sort of private ambulance.

During the long journey he worked out that he had two companions. They kept the bandages in place the entire time, but fed him sandwiches and bottled water at intervals.

"I guess there's no movie then?" he said, fishing for some sort of response. None was forthcoming.

He tried to engage them in conversation several times, even resorting to current affairs and the weather, but he was completely ignored. They were well trained.

To kill time, he plotted an elaborate escape plan, involving a comfort break, a packed lunchbox and a hypodermic needle, but in truth, his heart wasn't in it. Not yet, at least. It was too soon and there were too many unknown factors. Moreover, in his current condition, he wouldn't stand a chance against his two guards. This wasn't a comic book and he wasn't a superhero ... correction, supervillain. Hero? Villain? Who fucking knew anymore?

Potential typecasting aside, there was also the possibility that he might actually enjoy his new role. Maybe not long-term, but for a while.

Given the winding and, at times, uneven roads, the new facility must have been out in the countryside somewhere, at least a couple of hundred miles away from his previous home.

He was unloaded and whisked to new accommodation, where he was finally released from the muted darkness.

His new room was quite a bit bigger than the last. It had a high ceiling and a large sash window, throwing bright winter sunshine into the room. The furniture looked like it had been stolen from a stately home and included a comfortable king size bed and an antique writing desk.

He turned to see a wide-chested security type in a white polo shirt eying him. "Yes, this will do nicely, my good man," Han said and flashed a cheeky smile.

Rolling his eyes, the guard said, "You'll find that the wardrobe and drawers have been stocked with clothes and the en-suite has your toiletries."

"There's an en-suite too?"

The guard ignored the remark. "I'll let you get settled. Gabriel will be in to see you in half an hour."

***

After a light tap on the door, Gabriel entered Han's new quarters. As with their previous encounters, he was dressed in a grey suit and raincoat. With an affable smile, he said, "Hello, Han, how are you settling in?"

Han had been inspecting the clothing he had been provided with. Formal and informal day and evening wear, overalls, training gear, fatigues. They had planned for every eventuality. It was all very bland and perfunctory – not a movie t-shirt in sight. With an approving nod, he said, "Very well, thanks – love the new room. Not my usual choice in clothing, but no supermarket tat in sight either."

"You'll find that we spare no expense around here. We always ensure that you have the best tools for the job. We don't expect a task to be just completed. It has to be completed to our exacting requirements."

Han chose to let the last sentence slide for now. Instead, with a smile, he said, "It's almost like I have sponsorship now. I should have *Just Kill It* on my t-shirt, eh?"

"It could catch on." Gabriel cast his coat over a chair then clapped his hands together. "This is where the hard work really begins. This is one of our training facilities. We have the best instructors in the world in CQB, weapons and field craft. You were good at what you do, but we're going to make you much better."

Visions of Tom Cruise and Tom Skerritt sprang to mind. Han raised an eyebrow and opened his mouth to speak, but Gabriel held up a hand, saying, "We have a file on you as thick as War and Peace and I've read it cover to cover … three times. I probably know a lot more about you than your friend, Perry ever did."

Han could not quite hide the involuntary flinch at the mention of his dead best friend.

"I'm sorry to mention him," Gabriel said in earnest. "I know how close the two of you were." Returning to his point, he said, "I know all of your current strengths and limitations. I know about the CP and surveillance training by the boys in Durham and the few jobs you got off the back of it, your short stint in the RMP Reserve and every club, school and gym you've ever attended and what courses you took and what grades you achieved. You're a proficient street fighter – mainly mixed martial arts and boxing – and capable with a limited array of small arms, blunt and edged weapons."

"You're going to make me blush."

"We will make you an expert in all of those areas and in quite a few others as well. All forms of small arms, explosives, poisons, counter surveillance." He shrugged. "You get the picture."

"I do. I just don't know whether I truly believe it yet. I guess I'll be more of an Alec Trevelyan than James Bond though, eh?"

"I was waiting for a film reference," Gabriel said with an amused shake of the head. "It's something of a modus operandi for you, isn't it?"

"You could say that." His tone turning serious, Han said, "Why? Why me? Surely, what I can do for you can't possibly stack up against the enormous expense of saving my life, along with all the training, equipment, board, lodgings etcetera. And that's not even touching on all the trouble you've all gone to at significant risk. Wouldn't it be cheaper and easier to recruit and then control some sort of ex-SAS mercenary team? You know, some Wild Geese or Dogs of War type guys?"

"If we were operating beyond our own borders, yes, I would agree wholeheartedly. Ex-military guns for hire would be the way forward. But this is an internal battle we're fighting and as such, a completely different kettle of fish. Our 'soldiers' have to be subversive guerrillas, operating within the bounds of normal life. They have to be able to coexist with the very people that we are trying to weed out. They need to stay under the radar until needed and then slip back under it afterwards."

"I didn't quite achieve that though, did I?"

"You managed on your own for over two years whilst clocking up one of the highest individual body counts this country has ever known. Possibly *the* highest. With the support of this organisation, there will be no limits to your achievements." As an afterthought, he added, "As long as you can be a team player."

Han resisted the urge to roll his eyes. "Naturally."

"As for the trouble and significant risk," Gabriel said, "it was actually a fairly straight forward retrieval for us."

Gabriel appeared to study him for a time and then added, "With that said, you do represent a sizeable investment on our part, so we do intend to protect that investment every step of the way."

"Yes, I get it," Han said, a little tetchiness slipping through.

"I'm sorry to bang on about it," Gabriel replied, holding his hands up. "After what happened with your father, the Board are understandably concerned and eager to reassert complete control."

"The bastard murdered my mum and my best friend. You don't have to remind me."

Changing the subject, Gabriel said, "I'm told your training will begin after lunch. You will be assigned a lead instructor who will plan and coordinate your training schedule."

"Can we not skip this part of the story with a montage?"

Gabriel laughed. "That would actually be really useful and save us all a lot of time, but unfortunately this is the real world."

"I'm not so sure."

Shaking his head, Gabriel grabbed his coat and held out his hand. "I have to go unfortunately. I would've liked to have stuck around for your first day of training, but meetings have to be attended and reports have to be written. My life is playing out in dull shades of grey in comparison to yours, Han."

Han grasped the man's hand and shook it. He had a solid grip – a man who hadn't always worn a suit and tie. Was Gabriel some sort of ex-spook? He had to have been recruited from somewhere himself at some point. Military intelligence would be high up on the list of possibilities.

"Some of us just have all the fun, eh?" Han said with a wink.

***

After a high energy, nutritious lunch in a deserted canteen big enough for a primary school, one of the polo shirt orderlies instructed him to get changed into a tracksuit and trainers and then meet his lead instructor in the entrance hall.

His instructor turned out to be a tall and athletic German called Amwolf. Han couldn't help himself. "Is that a piss-take?"

"I do not understand," the instructor said with a frown.

"Am wolf. Am serial killer," Han said and couldn't suppress a laugh.

"Amwolf translates from German to Eagle Wolf," he replied without a shred of humour.

Han stopped mid-laugh. Okay, this was going to be fun.

"It is time for your first session," Amwolf said evenly. "I will put you through your paces today and then, based on your performance, I will tailor a training regime for you."

"Sounds like a blast."

***

34

Five hours later, Han collapsed onto his bed, gasping and bleeding. He thought the ass-kicking he got from *The Weare* and his dad was bad, but that had been a tea party with Great Aunt Maude compared to Amwolf. Every inch of his body was battered and bruised. Cuts and abrasions separated the bruises from joining into one super-bruise. His drilled foot and replacement knee were both especially tender, making every limping step back to his room agony.

The session had started with a swim in the local lake – fully clothed. The water was cold and choked with reeds, water-lilies and crowfoot. Amwolf had, in his deadpan manner, also explained about the eels.

After the dunking, Han then warmed up with a cross-country run through the estate, his sodden trainers squelching with oozing mud. Following the run, he was then led to a wooded area that concealed an assault course.

Skipping obstacles was not allowed, regardless of how many failed attempts. He just had to keep throwing himself at them until sheer bloody-minded resolve managed to get him through.

Barely able to walk, the fun then really began. Amwolf took him through dozens of offensive and defensive one on one hand-to-hand combat scenarios. This was basically an excuse for Amwolf to kick the shit out of him for his earlier wisecracks. Han was not just a well-trained fighter, he was also instinctive, but he had nothing on Amwolf. This fucker should have been in the ring. He would've pissed all over any of those ultimate fighter guys.

No fun playing with guns or high explosives for Han. Not yet. Just a good old-fashioned beasting.

He lay still, his laboured breaths sending spikes of pain through his chest. As he closed his eyes, his mind turned to Cara. She was out there somewhere, rebuilding her life, moving on. The thought hurt more than the beasting. When he had finished the slaughter on *The Weare* he really had thought that he and Cara could have gone on to live a normal life together and that he could finally put the whole experiment – both phases – behind him. That pleasant delusion had lasted all of five minutes. In hindsight, he should have known that there would be no going back to a normal life, not after everything he had done and everything he had been through.

Charlie had brought him crashing back down to Earth, followed quickly by Will Wright. *Oh, what a night*, as the song went.

A thought occurred to him. Maybe he could get back in touch … Immediately, even as he was thinking it, he said aloud, "Don't be so fucking stupid." His voice bristled with bitter anger and seemed to bounce around the confines of the room, taunting him. No matter how much or how deeply she had once loved him, she would turn him in to the police in a heartbeat. She might be a little conflicted in doing it, but she would do the right thing – it was part of her charm. God damn it.

Maybe with his new face he could … His eyes snapped open and stared up at the ceiling. "Listen to yourself," he muttered with a snort. That sort of bullshit only worked in superhero films. The jury was still out, but he was pretty sure that he was more Peyton Westlake than Peter Parker. Either way, that shit definitely wouldn't float. A pair of glasses or a rubber mask just wouldn't cut the mustard in real life. *You look so familiar … oh fuck it, just kiss me … upside-down, if you can manage it …* His face had been altered here and there, but she would still recognise him immediately.

Cara had been the one good thing in his life – the one honest and decent thing – and it was over. Full stop. She had been the one thing worth having a 'normal' life for. Now that was no longer possible, what would he do? *No chance of a normal life, so let's just have a totally fucked up one instead? Really?* There was nothing holding him back. Would he just go along with Gabriel and these Troy Consortium cronies and become some sort of undercover assassin just because he had nothing better to do? His old life was over – all traces of the video shop owner were gone – Movie Maniac … gone. His home … gone. His mum … gone. Cara … gone. Jumanji …

He could almost feel the shift in the bed as Ju would wake up and shuffle up towards him. He could almost feel the brush of his soft fur against his hand, followed by the nudge of his cold nose, craving attention … affection. He could feel it … almost.

Hopefully Cara would have taken him in. He would have been beside himself when he hadn't returned. He would've felt abandoned, confused, unloved. *Ah, Ju, I'm sorry, buddy. I do still love you. I hope somehow on some level you still know that.*

In the end though, even Ju was gone to him. There was nothing left except Han.

Han had started out as an off the cuff undercover identity to use in Haydon and then throw away like a used condom once he was done with the experiment. But the identity had stuck. Those months in Haydon irreparably changed him and that let Han loose. Han had then gradually taken over, bit by bit until only his family, Cara and Perry were all that were anchoring him to his original persona. Cara was gone, Perry was dead, his mum was dead. Karl was still alive, but he would be utterly disgusted with what his little brother had done. And could he blame him? Karl couldn't possibly even begin to understand. Maybe if he knew the truth about their father, but that was never going to happen.

Gabriel had already explained to him that the Consortium had done a sterling job of erasing or muddying the link between Charlie and him, other than their online partnership to rid the world of scumbags. DCI Carter's testimony of the fragments of conversation she had overheard was uncorroborated and, after some sneaky DNA tampering by the Consortium ruled it out, she was ultimately ignored.

No, his brother would never understand. He probably still wouldn't turn him in though. Instead, he would beg him to turn himself in, rather than betray him, even after everything that he had done. If that ever happened it would cost Karl dearly – it could destroy his life. No, it was better that his brother continued to think him dead as well. No anchors left. Han was free …

So, when all was said and done, he really did have nothing better to do. Fuck it, he would just play ball. Until something better came along.

Goodbye, Cara. Goodbye, Ju. Goodbye, bro.

***

Bathed in shadows, in the narrow pathway between two modest semi-detached houses, a man watched and waited. The object of his attention had just returned home next door. The young Pakistani woman had unloaded the car and was struggling with several bulky shopping bags.

She reached the front door and set the bags down. As she rummaged in her shoulder bag for her keys, she clicked her tongue in irritation. The external wall light had not come on, as it should have, so she was fumbling in the dark. The house was in complete darkness; Asif would not be back from the mosque for another hour.

The man, known to some as Lionheart, continued to observe, as motionless as a stalking lioness in the long grass. Apart from one or two living room lights, the rest of the cul-de-sac was devoid of life. It took another drawn out minute for the Saracen to find the key. As she unlocked the door, he heard an approaching car.

Without a second to lose, he dashed out of the shadows and shoved the woman into the hallway. She fell back against the newel post at the bottom of the staircase, jolting her back and emitting a startled whimper. Slamming the door behind him, he drew out the silver dagger with the red cross on its hilt from under his long coat.

The woman opened her mouth to scream, but Lionheart sprang forward, clamping a hand over her mouth. He pressed the tip of the dagger against her throat, drawing a trickle of blood that traced the line of her throat down to the collar of her white blouse.

"One sound ... one movement ... and I will not only kill you, but I will also butcher your entire family, beginning with your husband and then your parents." The looming man's tone was a low guttural rumble that was matter-of-fact and emotionless. His eyes seemed to glow in the darkness, as if daring her to disobey.

She was shaking uncontrollably and her eyes were stretched impossibly wide, but she remained silent, save for her gasping breaths.

"Good girl," Lionheart said.

With practiced ease, he taped her mouth and hands and then dragged her up the stairs by her prim ponytail. He threw her onto the bed and then stared at her small boyish frame.

Her eyes darted about the room, desperately searching for something – *anything* – to help her. Her eyes quickly returned to her attacker. The bear of a man stood over her and gently stroked his goatee beard. As he stepped to the edge of the bed, the dagger seemed to shimmer in the starlight seeping in through the window.

He watched her in silence for a moment, seemingly soaking up her anguish and discomfort. "Your unholy jihad against the crusader ends tonight, bitch."

Her eyes widened further and she shook her head fiercely. Her mouth worked to form words beneath the tape, but they came out hopelessly muffled. She shuffled up the bed, contracting into a ball against the headboard.

"I will not listen to any of your black lies. Your husband is an active member of the Islamic Fundamentalist group, Hizb ut Tahrir and a Saracen. He will die by my blade."

She was shaking her head with tears streaming down her face.

Leaning closer, his top lip quivering, he added, "As a collaborator, you are equally guilty, you Babylonian whore."

The woman screamed with such force that the tape started working loose. Irritated, he raised the dagger and brought the cross hilt down hard on the bridge of her slender nose. The bone splintered with a loud crack and blood oozed from the deep laceration.

She slumped back, dazed and weeping softly.

He glanced at the droplets of blood spattered on the white bed linen then back to the moaning woman.

He reached down and dragged her skirt up over her thighs as she squirmed and kicked. Leaning close to her bleeding face, he said, "There is only one way to treat a whore."

***

A car pulled onto the drive, parking parallel to the first. A couple of minutes later the front door opened and a young man's voice said, "Ayesha, I'm home."

The house was quiet and in darkness. The slim man lifted his glasses to rub his tired eyes then hung his keys on a hook by the door. Frowning, he craned his head to look up the stairs. "Ayesha? Are you in bed already?"

He turned back to the kitchen and caught a glimpse of shopping bags on the worktops, but before he could process it properly a soft thump from above caught his attention. With a sigh, he climbed the stairs slowly, his cotton thobe rustling with each step. At the top of the stairs, he stared at the open doorway of the bedroom. "Ayesha, are you alright?"

He stepped up to the door and his eyes fell upon the bloodied naked body of his wife, splayed out across the bed. She was bleeding from between her wide-open legs and the crumpled covers were stained and smeared around her motionless form. His brain struggled to process the appalling scene, the unimaginable horror of it skewering him like a harpoon.

After a moment's dumbfounded hesitation, he shrieked and rushed forward. He immediately felt a searing pain in his side.

Lionheart stepped out from behind the door, bloodied dagger in hand.

Asif clutched his side. Blood was staining the cream fabric red from where Lionheart's dagger had pierced his flesh as he passed him. Despite the pain, Asif stumbled towards the bed, ignoring the intruder. "Ayesha! No, please!" Reaching the edge of the bed, he caught sight of the gaping wound across her throat. Her lifeless glass-like eyes stared unblinking up at the ceiling. Pain and anguish were carved deep into her features. A mixture of nausea and despair brought him to his knees beside his dead wife. A strangled sob choked his throat as he clutching at her limp outstretched hand. There was still some residual warmth in it, but it was ebbing away fast, and the colour along with it.

"It is your time to die, Saracen," Lionheart said, stepping up behind him.

Asif wrenched his eyes away from Ayesha and turned to face his wife's murderer, staring up into piercing eyes. He made no effort to defend himself. He was already dead inside.

Lionheart slipped the tip of the dagger into the base of his skull and thrust forward. The man twitched once and then was gone.

Gripping the man's hair, Lionheart drew the blade back out and let the man fall to the ground. He stared at the man and then his dead wife. It lacked his usual elegance, but it was still a good clean kill.

His eyes lingered on the whore's open legs, drawing his attention up to her ruined private parts. He had washed her filthy juices off his manhood, but her scent lingered. He savoured it and smiled.

It's time.

CHAPTER 4

True to his word, Amwolf prepared a rigorous training schedule and aggressively ensured that Han hit each and every goal. He was introduced to several other instructors specialising in various subjects, including firearms, explosives, covert entry and surveillance. In between classes, practical exercises and firing ranges, Amwolf continued his beatings and physical exercise regime.

After a twelve hour day, Han would shower and then promptly collapse on his bed. Due to mental and physical exhaustion, most of the time he slept like the dead. Dreamless. But the times when sleep's loving embrace did not take him immediately, thoughts of Cara would ease back into his fatigued mind. Sometimes she would be joined by Karl or Ju, but Cara would be ever-present.

***

Han sat in the canteen, wisps of steam rising from his damp and grimy tracksuit. A high protein pasta dish lay in front of him. He held a fork in his trembling hand, but could not summon the willpower to load it. His heart felt like it was going to beat its way through his ribcage. It was only lunchtime and he already felt like a corpse.

How long could his body take this punishment? He wasn't as young as he used to be. He was getting stronger with every passing day and, although his various injuries pained him, especially towards the end of each shift, they weren't holding him back. As a counterpoint to the unending torture, he was continuing to receive the best in sports and injury physiotherapy. No matter how horrible it was the previous day, somehow the massages and manipulations managed to help him just enough to drag his weary ass back out of bed to do it all over again.

The concoction of vitamins, drugs, high protein bars and carefully selected meals were clearly helping. The meals weren't exactly the most mouth-watering or exciting cuisine, but they filled a gap. To be honest, there were times when he would have eaten a dead horse, and he wasn't talking about a frozen lasagne either.

As he sat, locked in a battle of wills with the fork, a man entered the canteen. He wasn't one of the regular polo shirt brigade. He was tall and, despite the long coat, Han could sense a powerful frame beneath. His goatee and olive skin gave him a Mediterranean appearance. The man glanced in his direction and their eyes met. Han recognised the look of a predator immediately. There was a burning intensity behind those eyes.

Han offered him a cheery smile, but he just turned away. Curious, Han continued to watch him. The man took a fistful of pills with a bottle of water, but didn't bother with food. Still standing, he chased the pills with a gulp of water then strode back out the way he came.

Their eyes locked once more then the man was gone.

There was no need for Han to speculate on the man's role in the Consortium.

***

After three months of intensive training, Han was led through the forest into a clearing that was new to him. A shallow pond lay at its centre, the rain bouncing off the surface like the skin of a drum.

Darkness was descending fast, the last of the long shadows already in rapid retreat.

Both Han and Amwolf were already drenched from the cross-country run. Steam rose from their bodies, betraying the exertion they had both already endured.

They were alone and several miles from the house.

As he stood at the water's edge, the cold and wet drove a shiver across Han's shoulders. He glanced around the gloomy clearing, taking in the woodland scents deep into his lungs. He caught a hint of wild garlic. Regulating his breathing, he said, "This place is new. What fun surprise do you have in store for me now?"

"You are improving daily," Amwolf said as he walked purposefully into the water, rain cascading around him.

"Why thank you, Master Yoda."

Amwolf stepped into the middle of the pond. With muddy water lapping at his thighs, he stretched his neck from side to side and said, "You are ready."

"Ready for what?" Han swiped away the rainwater running down his face and folded his arms. "Have you got some kind of killer robot for me to take down?" Han managed a tired laugh.

Amwolf shook his head. "No, just me."

Han opened his mouth to speak. They had fought on many occasions and Amwolf had always won. Recently, Han had come very close a few times though.

Amwolf cut him off. "You must best me in this … teich … pond. If you do not I will kill you."

Han studied the man's pale dripping face as the rain continued relentlessly. He wasn't joking or being melodramatic. He was deadly serious.

"That would be a bit of a waste of the Consortium's money and resources though, wouldn't it?"

"If you are not ready now you will never be and therefore there is no point in wasting any further time on you."

Han opened his mouth, but instead of speaking, he looked up into the black sky and let rainwater fall onto his tongue. He savoured it for a time and then, with a reluctant shrug, he began walking into the freezing water.

Almost immediately, his trainers began sinking into thick oozing mud and it became a struggle to drag his feet out with each step.

As he approached, Amwolf said, "To survive, you must utilize what you have learned. You will not win through instinctive fighting alone. You must think also."

As Han slowly made his way towards his teacher, his mind raced with options, ideas, scenarios, mentally flicking through the overflowing rolodex of his mind. Absently, it occurred to him that it was about time that he computerised his mental systems. His trainers were being sucked off his feet and, as he drew within striking distance, his first key decision was made. He forced his trainers off and left them behind, but continued to move forward as if still restricted by them.

Amwolf stepped to one side. Han realised that he wasn't staying in one spot for long and he moved like he had possibly removed his shoes as well. Moving about was preventing him from sinking into the mud.

He processed everything in seconds and, predicting his next step, Han moved in to intercept. Amwolf anticipated the move and blocked Han's first two blows. He countered with a jab to Han's ribs that forced him back. He managed to block Amwolf's second and third blows as he backtracked.

"Good start, but you did not consider that I was leading you to attack me where I wanted you."

Wheezing, Han said, "You're too kind, mate."

"Again."

Amwolf tracked around the edge of the pond, where it was only ankle deep. Han moved to intercept, taking his time, getting his breath back. His rib was starting to throb – the bastard might have cracked it.

As Han closed in Amwolf came at him, impossibly fast, given the mud. It caused Han to start and back up.

Amwolf kept coming, but at the last moment switched direction, causing Han to attack the air and exposing his side once more. Amwolf angled back in and punched him in the ribs again. Same rib. A definite crack that time.

Han staggered backwards and almost lost his footing on a branch or stone hidden beneath the surface. "Fucker," he spat and clutched at his side.

"Not good enough," Amwolf said as he continued to move. "At this rate, I will kill you. Do you want to die, Han?"

"Fuck you!"

Amwolf's usually calm expression turned suddenly angry. "Do you want to *die*? You *will* die right here, if you do not use everything you know and everything you can. Now come at me, otherwise I will kill you where you stand, like the coward that you are!"

As the rain fell between them, Han made his second key decision. He quelled his rising anger, but screamed in rage and rushed at Amwolf with artificial rage etched into his features.

He caught a flicker of disappointment in Amwolf's eyes as he readied himself.

Instead of attacking him head on, Han dove into the water at Amwolf's feet. Before Amwolf could process what was happening, Han wedged his head between his instructor's feet and rammed his shoulders against the man's shins, throwing him off balance and stumbling forward.

Han launched himself upwards, further unbalancing his opponent and causing him to collapse onto his knees. He then spun and fell upon him as he turned to greet him. Muddy water lashed up around them, obscuring both men's vision.

Han managed to connect a cross against the side of Amwolf's head before he recovered and unleashed a barrage of blows into Han's face and rolled Han onto his back.

Han's face disappeared beneath the surface and he sucked in several gulps of gritty water before rolling away and resurfacing briefly to gasp at the air.

Amwolf was upon him once more, kicking at his exposed replacement knee. The pain was excruciating, causing Han to scream out and clutch at the injured area.

Forcing the pain aside, Han rolled away then jumped to his feet, favouring his injured leg. Amwolf had tracked around to the side, so was not in the position he thought he would be.

Han spun to see him coming at him once more. This time he managed to block his initial onslaught, but lost ground in the process. He fell back right to the water's edge.

The ground was firmer at the edge, so Han used it, moving quickly to one side, then back, before finally launching himself at Amwolf. His teacher managed to block the attack by using Han's own momentum against him and throwing him past him back into the centre of the pond. Han sprawled face down in the water, arms flapping.

The attack had managed to unbalance Amwolf and he slipped as he turned, dropping to his knees briefly.

Han rolled then found his feet once more, coughing up stagnant water. Amwolf's stumble had cost him a quick counterattack, so instead he was coming at him more deliberately.

Han was breathing heavily and wincing with every movement of his injured knee and ribs. His nose and lips were bleeding and his left eye was starting to swell. Amwolf appeared composed and untouched. This was not looking good.

The rain continued to fall, washing rivulets of blood down Han's ashen face.

Amwolf did not allow him any time to reflect. He came at him one more time and something in his set expression confirmed that this would be the final attack. Han moved forward to meet him, grim resolve set into his own features.

This time Han lurched forward, but pulled back short of contact. Amwolf came with him and Han pivoted and used his shoulder to take him down. Water splashed into his eyes, but he kept hold of his teacher and plunged him beneath the surface.

Amwolf squirmed and fought like a crocodile on acid, writhing and thrashing. Blows and counter-holds emerging out of nowhere. Han felt pain from several new places, but maintained his grip, unaware that he was snarling, "Fucker ... stay ... fucking ... down ..."

Amwolf's legs managed to slip around Han's and suddenly he was on his back, gulping water once more. He surfaced, coughing and blinded, but kept fighting.

They grapple once more, exchanging several blows. Han's lungs felt ready to explode and his legs about to fold beneath him. He felt an abrupt detachment to his own body and the sucking mud that had been dragging at his feet like concrete seemed to fall away from him.

Just as exhaustion threatened to overwhelm him completely, suddenly Amwolf staggered back from the fray and held up a hand. "Enough," he said, drawing in deep breaths.

They stared at each other for a time, just the splashing rain and their laboured breaths disturbing the night.

It took several minutes for Han's faintness to fade and for the clarity to return to every leaf and splash of rain. Finally, Han managed to say, "So ... do I get to fight another day?"

Amwolf stared at him and gradually a smile played across his bloodied lips.

***

After the Battle of the Pond, Han's training drew to a close. He had put on nearly two stone of muscle, his cheek did indeed now resemble an ugly birth defect and the rest of his injuries were mere stains on the bed sheets of history, apart from the missing fingers, of course, and the occasional twinge in his right foot. He had also picked up a few more scars during training to sit proudly alongside those acquired from Haydon, *The Weare* and a certain dead Royal Marine Commando.

Staring at his toned, muscular torso in the mirror, Han raised his eyes and smiled. He had never been in such good shape. Ever. He didn't mind the scars either, in fact, he growing kind of fond of them. They added ... character. He considered them trophies; hard fought and well earned.

He slipped on a plain white t-shirt that hugged his frame. *Plain white?* He clicked his tongue. He had never been a white t-shirt kinda guy. He had missed his old wardrobe from day one, but it was beginning to get obsessional. Thoughts of his first online shopping spree at the likes of *Last Exit to Nowhere* or *Nerdoh* sometimes filled his mind as he would eat his dinner or take a shower. He would imagine all the new and insightful designs that they may now have available for old and new films alike.

His uninspiring wardrobe would be the first thing to redress on his release back into the wild. He would be placing orders wholesale.

His thoughts were interrupted by a light tap on the door. Han recognised Gabriel's knock. "Come in, Gabe."

"How are you doing, Han?" Gabriel asked, walking into the room. "You look good."

"We've been through this – you're not my type," Han quipped.

Gabriel smiled and pushed his hands into his coat pockets. "How do you feel? Are you ready for this? To get back out there?"

There seemed genuine concern in his tone. Han was touched. Well, more surprised than touched. He faced him, folded his arms and contemplated the questions. He refrained from saying, *spare me, Burke, I've already had my psych evaluation this month*. Instead, with conviction, he said, "Yes, I'm ready."

Gabriel studied the man for a time and then nodded slowly. "Yes, I believe you are." He pulled his coat off and sat down, draping the coat over his lap and indicating Han to sit as well.

Han took the desk chair and spun to face him, his expression expectant.

Getting straight to business, Gabriel said, "We're going to set you up with a rented apartment in London. You'll be provided with everything you need, including identification, a bank account with starting funds of £10,000 and a monthly salary of £5,000. Your apartment will be kitted out with all the essentials, so your starting balance can be used however you wish – new wardrobe or whatever. Your salary is then for everything else, including incidental expenses for assignments. Any assignments that require additional funds over and above normal expenses will be authorised by me and transferred into your account as and when you need them. If any specialist equipment is needed for an assignment we will of course provide it for you, including weapons, vehicles and explosives."

Han listened intently as Gabriel continued, "You're not going to be on a banker's salary, but £5,000 is more than adequate, so we expect you to live within your means. You may from time to time be entitled to bonuses based on performance, which will be authorised by the Board on my recommendation."

Han leaned back in his chair and whistled. "Performance? Expenses? Bonuses?" He shook his head, adding, "It sounds like I'm taking on a sales rep job."

"Just because our service is a little on the *exotic* side it doesn't mean that we're any less diligent when it comes to operational procedures or financial budgets. We still account for everything; we pay our taxes and we have backers that need to see a return on their investment."

"Who are these backers?"

"That is not your concern and it never will be. Certain members of the Board are the only people privy to that information."

Han didn't pursue it any further. He had an idea of who at least some of the investors might be. Changing the subject, he said, "So what's my job? My assignments? My cover?"

Gabriel smiled. "I think you'll like the life we've created for you. A lot of thought went into it – we wanted it to be something you would buy into and something that you already have a working knowledge of."

"Oh, you tease," Han said, smiling. "Do tell!"

"You're going to be a freelance writer. You already have dozens of articles to your name and even a regular column in the Evening Standard."

"And one unpublished novel," Han added. He meant the remark as a joke, but he failed to find any humour in it. Disregarding it, he added, "I have been busy."

Gabriel either didn't notice the briefest flicker of a change in mood with Han or he chose not to comment. Continuing, he said, "We have someone who is writing for you. It's your favourite subject – films."

That was enough to vanquish the threat of a sullen mood. Han burst out laughing. "You're kidding?" Clapping his hands, he added, "I've always considered myself a silent film critic, but now I will actually have a voice."

Smiling, Gabriel raised a hand and said, "Well, our anonymous writer has the voice, but yes, you are a film critic. I'll be giving you a comprehensive dossier on the life that we have constructed for you, including all the articles and comments that you have ever written. It is vitally important that you familiarise yourself with every aspect of your new life. You need to know even the smallest details like the back of your hand. This is essential to your reintroduction."

"Won't someone who writes for the Evening Standard be known already?"

"No – the man you are going to become is a recluse. He … you never do live or face to face interviews, you works from home and you avoid the social scene."

"I sound like a boring twat," Han said with a smirk.

"For our purposes, boring is good. Boring is under the radar and inconspicuous."

Han frowned. "How long has this ghost writer been writing as me?"

"Since your retrieval, so he has already had a chance to build up a body of work for you."

"You really do think of everything." With a shrug, he asked, "So what about the assignments?"

"They will usually be sent to you by courier. The target could be anywhere in the UK and you may receive one in three months or two in one week – there are no set limits or restrictions. We won't overwork you though – you can be assured of that. For one, too many targets in a small period of time risks drawing attention from the wrong people and that is precisely what we do not want."

"And what determines a legitimate target around here?" It wasn't a question he'd usually ask, but he felt in some small way that he was still in Phase Two mode.

"Again, that is not your concern." Gabriel leant forward, his hands clasped tightly together. "But let me assure you that each target will represent a very real danger to the United Kingdom.

Each target is investigated thoroughly and then assessed by a panel of experts before being assigned."

"One final question," Han said, standing up.

Gabriel eased back and folded his arms. For the first time in their association, Han caught a glimmer of disquiet. It was banished in an instant. "Sure."

"When do I start?" Han said with a wink.

Gabriel stood up and grasped Han's hand. "That's the spirit. We're going to let you bed in to your new life for a month or two. Take the time to ease into your new environment and to learn everything about your cover. Then, when you're settled, you'll be sent your first assignment."

On the way out, Gabriel explained, "I will be in touch regularly, but we will only meet every three months or so for one to ones. The meets will always take place at secure Consortium locations and every precaution will be taken to ensure mine and the Consortium's complete anonymity."

Amwolf greeted them at the front door. His muscular arms were folded across his chest and his expression was cold indifference. But as Han drew close, he smiled and held out a hand. "I am proud of you, my friend," he said in earnest.

Han was taken aback for a moment, eyes widening at what was a profoundly gracious gesture from the normally stone-faced German. He cast the surprise aside and shook the man's hand vigorously. "Thanks, mate. You pushed damn hard, but it was worth every minute of pain. You're the man, Am."

Gabriel smiled at the exchange and then shook Han's hand one final time. "Good luck my ... what was is it again ... Padawan?"

Han laughed. "Aye, that's right. I'll no doubt speak to you soon."

***

Han was chauffeured to London in a private car. He tried to engage the driver in some light-hearted banter, but his responses were strictly monosyllabic. Most of his personal effects had been sent on ahead, so he only had a rucksack with him as he stood on the curb outside his Camberwell apartment block, overlooking Burgess Park.

The apartment block looked pleasant enough, set in a quiet residential neighbourhood. It wasn't exactly central London, but he supposed the 'burbs fitted more with his solitary lifestyle.

He had never been a big fan of London – nice to visit, but had never had the inclination to live there. But this is where he had been sent, so he would just have to get on with it. The Troy Consortium had provided everything for him, including a very reasonable chunk of cash and monthly salary. He could rough it with the middle classes for a while.

As the car pulled away, Han waved and was rewarded with a curt nod from the driver. Then he was on his own. Just the way he liked it. Of course, that was an illusion. They would be keeping tabs on him continuously.

An unsettling feeling of agoraphobia washed over him. He resisted the urge to call after the car, but his eyes lingered on it, long after it had disappeared from sight.

After months of being cooped up on the training estate, it felt strange to be back out in the real world. He still associated that world with his old life. He was yet to do anything in this brave new world as the new and improved Han Mark II, so everything felt quite alien to him.

A sudden image flashed before his eyes of Brooks Hatlen, stepping outside the gates of Shawshank prison for the first time, terrified and alone. Red's voice seemed to drift on the gentle breeze … *He should've died in here* …

He took in a few deep breaths, sampling the very essence of the area. The air was fresh and sweet. After a few minutes, it seemed to do the trick. The slight queasy sensation gradually ebbed away, leaving him composed and prepared.

Brooks had been wrong. It was a whole lot better being back on the outside.

His apartment had two bedrooms. The smaller of the two had been set up as an office, complete with a top of the range laptop and printer. The kitchen and bathroom were small and perfunctory, but, like the office, they were kitted out with high spec appliances. The moderately sized living room was also well equipped with two leather sofas and a wall-mounted flat screen television. It was a mere 32 inches, so it would not do, but it was a nice gesture.

He had ten grand in the bank, so he started making a mental shopping list; for the TV, something around the 50 inches department, and maybe throw in 3D too. *I don't mind if I do …*

He spent the next few days shopping. As well as tackling the television, he started to rebuild his previous DVD collection with Blu-Rays, bought an iPhone, docking station and downloaded a few dozen choice albums to get it started. His wardrobe got the makeover it so desperately desired, with a host of film t-shirts, Converse All Stars and a leather jacket. He also decorated the walls and windowsills with some framed film prints – Silence of the Lambs (not his prized signed image of Hannibal Lecter unfortunately), The Thing, Alien, Pulp Fiction, Get Carter, Blade Runner, Jaws and many more.

A couple of bottles of Jack Daniels finished the place off nicely.

It took some work, but the apartment was really starting to feel like home.

He sat eating a takeaway Singapore Chow Mein, sipping whiskey and watching the Bourne films back to back. *Call it research and for a spot of inspiration,* he mused. Half way through The Bourne Supremacy, his mobile launched into the John Carpenter score from Halloween.

He had a pretty good idea who it would be.

It was an unknown number, but Han said, "Hi, Gabe. How ya doing?"

"I'm fine, thanks, Han," Gabriel said, his tone mildly amused. "How are you enjoying the films?"

Han rolled his eyes – a typically unsubtle and unnecessary reminder. "I forgot how good they were. There's no doubt that they helped revive the Bond franchise. I haven't seen the Jeremy Renner one yet, so the jury's out on that one."

"How are you settling in? London must be a bit of a change."

"Suburbia is suburbia wherever you are," Han said and sipped some of his whiskey. "But the apartment is comfortable, thanks."

"I'm glad to hear it. While you settle in, keep familiarising yourself with your new life. Every time the ghostwriter submits a new piece of work to the paper, you will receive a copy too, so make sure you read each new piece, as well as the back catalogue. You need to keep on top of it." Gabriel paused briefly then continued, saying, "Your laptop has been set up with an email account for the newspaper and a private one for our purposes. You'll receive digital copies of your articles through this private email account. The ghostwriter has full access to your newspaper email account, so he will submit the work for you. He will also respond to other emails for you, but it will be important for you to still monitor this account so that you are aware of all the activity."

"Understood."

"We've secured your new iPhone, so feel free to use it. I'll text you a number that you can contact me on. Try not to use it unless you feel it is absolutely necessary."

"Okay." Han fought the urge to add 'whatever'. He liked the guy, but he came across as a bit of a school master when he was laying down the law. He was beginning to feel like a naughty child. Come to think of it, where was a naughty schoolgirl when you needed one? The thought threw up images of Cara and he felt his jaw tighten.

Oblivious to Han's sudden mood change, Gabriel said, "I'm sorry to go on about this stuff, but it's important to get off on the right foot."

"No problem," Han heard himself mutter.

"Alright, well, I'll leave you to your film."

Han managed a convincing *goodbye* then set the phone down.

He cast the remains of the takeaway into the bin and turned the film off. He took the bottle of Jack and his glass to the chair by the window. There he sat, lost in his thoughts, staring out into the darkness beyond.

The first thing we do, let's kill all the lawyers.

CHAPTER 5

Han spent the next few weeks getting into character and touring London. The getting into character part was easy enough – he felt an immediate affinity with his new film critic persona for obvious reasons.

There was one somewhat jarring niggle. He did not agree with all of his supposed views and reviews on certain films. For starters, how dare he slate the prequel to the The Thing! It was fair to say that it was more of a remake and plagiarised many elements from the original, but to point blank pan it was uncalled for.

Another archived review that he disagreed with was for Inglourious Basterds. No self-confessed movie fan could completely firebomb the great Tarantino. Perry would be doing summersaults in his grave. A balanced judgment could point out that it was not without flaws, most notably some of the self-indulgently over-extended scenes, but to call it 'a pain to sit through' was blasphemous.

On the plus side, at least his views on a certain sparkly vampire gravy train were on the money, so it wasn't all bad.

Even though he had visited London on several occasions, apart from the well-known touristy areas, the rest of central London might as well have been a foreign country.

So, Han spent a lot of time and foot rubber on familiarising himself with the lay of the land. He did a lot of walking, but also travelled on buses and the tube. The tube was as crowded as he remembered it to be and many of the people were ill-mannered and ill-tempered. There was a great deal of construction and redevelopment going on – final preparations for the coming Olympics – so there was a lot of disruption and noise, which only fuelled people's intolerances.

On a positive note, as there were people of all shapes, sizes, colours and creeds, his facial and hand disfigurements went largely unnoticed. When the occasional person did notice, Han couldn't help but feel a spike of irritation. He managed to hold his tongue though, for the sake of presenting a good impression for his new employers, rather than for public safety.

Yes, it was a fun old place that was more of a chore than a joy, but he did take in a couple of shows and visited many of the other must-do attractions. He particularly enjoyed the tranquillity and sedate pace of the London Eye. He spent the thirty minutes in blissful solitude, soaking up the stunning views.

Reading the Evening Standard one morning in a coffee shop overlooking Westminster Bridge on the bank of the Thames, he was somewhat taken aback to learn that the Haydon Northumberland massacre was going to be made into a two part television drama.

There was quite an uproar about it. Many people were arguing that it was far too soon to consider dramatising such a recent and appalling event. Comments ranged from immortalising a monster to profiteering off misery.

It was fair to call his *antics* in Haydon as that of a monster, but that was not what Han had mixed feelings about. It was quite an honour on one hand, but on the other, it was also a time of his life that he would rather forget.

There would also be some RADA-esq twat of an actor portraying him, method acting the shit out of himself to try to get inside his head. The inevitable goal being to reveal him as a one-dimensional evil fiend. How could someone possibly get inside his head to understand his inner workings? He hadn't given anyone a chance. Well, the only living exceptions that could even begin to comment would be Cara and Karl, but they would hardly involve themselves. On the plus side, there were whispers that Damien Lewis was up for the part. As long as they didn't settle for Phil Mitchell!

There would also be some young actress playing Lisa. She would be depicting her as the sexy, but damaged heroine. That would be even more difficult to see. There were no names attached to her role yet, but there was no one on Earth that could play Lisa.

And then, although not a major issue, there was finally the small fact that it was a drama ... for television. No Hollywood blockbuster then? It was stupid and egotistical, but it still left a sour taste in his mouth. They made feature films about insignificant killers like the Zodiac Killer, Aileen Wuornos and Henry Lee Lucas, but he had to be content with a television drama? There was at least three different films about that freak, Ed Gein, for God's sake. There was no justice in the world. Maybe Hollywood would take notice and do something about *The Weare*. That would make a good action thriller. One can only dream.

He had to smack himself in the side of the head to stop thinking about it. *Who the fuck do you think you are? Get over yourself, you prat.*

An aspiring J K Rowling tapping away on her laptop looked up and shot him an irritated glare.

His smile must have been a little more predatory than he wanted it to be because she quickly thrust her head back down and resumed typing without another glance.

He was beginning to wonder whether an assignment would ever materialise, that the whole thing had been some kind of extremely elaborate joke at his expense. That was absurd of course, but as time crept on, the intense training, Amwolf and Gabriel all began to blur into obscurity. Then, abruptly, his first assignment quite literally dropped into his lap. And with it, the new job became very real.

It was late afternoon and he was returning to his apartment building after a trip to Battersea Park and the old power station. A light drizzle of rain had started to fall when a courier thrust a package into his hand and then jumped back on a motorcycle and sped off.

Han stared after the bike for a moment then, clutching the package to his chest, he hurried inside.

A mixture of excitement and trepidation sent him straight to a bottle of Jack before opening the package. After knocking back one shot and refilling, he sat down at the desk and eyed the padded A4 envelope. He turned it over in his hands a couple of times. It was completely unmarked.

After another sip of Tennessee whiskey, he muttered, "Tally-ho" and ripped it open. The package contained a manila dossier stamped with FOR YOUR EYES ONLY.

Han rolled his eyes. *Someone is bloody loving this shit.* Whilst humming the theme song, he opened the folder and started reading its contents.

Tonight, Matthew, my target will be … Geoffrey Sanderson.

Han examined the handful of black and white photos of the target. He was tall and slim with glasses and a prominent nose. With thinning dark hair, he appeared around mid forties. Glancing at the summary page, he discovered that he was actually thirty-eight.

"Not ageing well, old bean," he said to no one in particular.

Continuing to read, he raised his eyebrows. A criminal defence barrister. Interesting. An expert with loopholes and legal precedents to help get scumbags off the hook. Makes sense then.

The dossier contained detailed information on the target's interests, routines, family and friends. It also listed his regular haunts, including work and home addresses and social hangouts.

After he finished reading the dossier, his initial excitement waned. He sat back and finished the glass of Jack, his expression thoughtful. When you set aside the Troy Consortium and all their resources, the reality was that this was just going over the same old ground. Yes, it was sexed up a bit, but it was still just Phase Two in a fur coat. *The Weare* had brought the tally up to the Phase One total. After that, he was then supposed to quit it all and enjoy a nice normal … ish life with Cara.

With a sigh, he said, "Well that all went tits up, so just fucking man up and get on with it." He then poured himself another whiskey.

***

Now that he was actually on an assignment, Han Whitman felt oddly exposed on the busy streets of central London. He became acutely aware of all the CCTV and additional security for the rapidly approaching Olympics Games. Police cars and foot patrols seemed to be waiting around every corner, not to mention the occasional army unit inspecting tower blocks for potential surface-to-air missile sites.

It was a fresh and cold morning with last night's rain filling potholes and gutters. It was the sort of morning where everyone was in a hurry, scurrying to work or on the school run. Buildings and roads had a grey sheen, which was matched by the dour faces of pedestrians and motorists.

He was dressed in an oversized winter coat, scarf and a newsboy cap pulled down, covering the top half of his face.

It wasn't his normal get up, but it was a reasonable plain sight disguise. Still, as he passed a couple of uniformed police officers pounding the beat, his heart managed a brief back flip.

He clearly wasn't himself yet. *Just gotta get back into the flow of things,* he kept telling himself. Get back on the horse. He may not be entirely overjoyed with being railroaded into the new job, but he didn't have a whole lot of choice in the matter and he had already established that he didn't have a hell of a lot else to do either. *Get your God damn game face on.*

Geoffrey Sanderson's chambers were on Fleet Street. Han had taken the tube to Charing Cross and walked up The Strand. The roads and pavements were choked with traffic, road works and pedestrians from all walks of life.

He experienced a sudden and vivid memory from his journey to Haydon at the very start of the experiment. He recalled an ASDA lorry roaring past in the outside lane on the motorway, spraying his old Peugeot with dirty surface water. *The ants scurrying to*

60

work or dropping the kids off at school. That had been Hannibal Whitman's birthday. On that journey, he had created the man who went on to gradually but completely take over from his previous persona.

He glanced around at the ants around him now. They still scampered about their dull and insignificant lives, worrying about the price of petrol, who to fuck and who to fuck-over. Nothing had changed. Nothing, except for him.

He caught sight of the building and, as luck would have it, there was a pub right across the street – Ye Olde Cock Tavern. *Christ, the fucking tourists must love that.*

Han headed straight for the pub without a second glance towards Sanderson's chambers.

Ye Olde Cock Tavern was narrow with bare flagstones on the floor and lots of dark wood and exposed brickwork. The smells of fresh coffee and old wood caught his attention. As he was on the job, so to speak, he grudgingly opted for a coffee. He then headed upstairs where he could sit at the window; a perfect vantage point to keep an eye on the other side of the road.

Han settled down with his coffee and fished out a Kindle e-book reader from his coat's inside pocket. He had remembered that wannabe hero guard reading one on *The Weare* and thought that he would give one a go. They would never steal the pleasure of reading a printed book – the crack of the spine, the smell of the paper – a proper book was a total sensory experience. But, fuck it, you had to move with the times. And, damn, it was much easier on the eye than he thought it would be as he started reading *The Hitchhiker's Guide to the Galaxy. Far out in the uncharted backwaters …*

As brilliant as Douglas Adams was, Han kept a close eye on the front door of the building across the street. There was a lot of comings and goings of mostly Joe Ordinary suit types, but not Geoffrey Sanderson.

He ordered a second coffee and a Danish pastry, more for effect than necessity. Arthur and Ford had just been picked up by the Heart of Gold when he caught sight of Sanderson leaving the building.

Han pocketed the Kindle, drained his coffee and headed downstairs. He left the pub in time to see Sanderson heading down towards The Strand. Han followed at a discreet distance.

This was an odd one for Han. His instructions were to make the hit look like an accident. *Hit?* Oh dear, he was sliding fast! It was clearly the Consortium testing their new recruit. In his murdering career, Han had not been a subtle killer. With Han's victims, there had never been any doubt that they had been murdered. Well, with the exception of one, his second victim, Tess 'Bet Marple' Runckle. But that irritating curtain-twitcher had been more by accident than design. He saw an opportunity and took it.

So, as nothing particularly inspiring had sprung to mind, his plan for Geoffrey Sanderson involved tailing him until some sort of opportunity arose. It wasn't exactly sophisticated or inspired, but it was all he had. London was, after all, a dangerous place.

Sanderson headed into the Strand Palace Hotel. Han followed, past the top-hatted porter and into an elegant contemporary lobby. Sanderson headed through into an expansive lounge bar and walked over to a corner table, where a man was already sat waiting.

Han sat at the bar and ordered yet another coffee. The thought of drinking a third in a row actually made him cringe. A pint of Guinness would've gone down far better. With a sigh, he took out his Kindle once more and watched the two men over the top of it.

The bar was quiet, only a scattering of punters and low chatter over the light jazz background music. It didn't take long for Han to clock a table with two stocky bodyguard types. They were keeping an eye on proceedings from a couple of tables away. Crew cuts, wide shoulders and cheap suits. Not very subtle.

Could this be a meeting with one of his sleazy clientele? Maybe he could pin his murder on them. No, the Consortium wanted an accident, not a murder. So an accident they would get. He had absolutely no idea how he would manage it, but he had to somehow.

The meeting ended with a handshake – it all appeared terribly civilised and above board, helped of course by the salubrious surroundings. The respectable face of modern organised crime – lunchtime meetings over lattes. Not exactly the romanticised picture from the movies of darkened smoke-filled rooms, full of hard-drinkers and hand cannons. Edward G Robinson would be clawing his way out of his grave to create some new surprised cadavers. Frank McCloud got his way after all … a world in which there's no place for Johnny Rocco.

Some people have youth, some have beauty … I have menace. Come back, Ed, all is forgiven. I'll buy you a box of Montecristos.

The yuppie mobster left first with his two Primark goons. Sanderson took his time. He finished his latte, adjusted his tie, sent a text message and then headed for the exit.

Han sighed and jammed the e-book reader back into his pocket. This was getting boring. He was having a nice little jaunt around central London, tailing the knob-jockey, but he was no closer to thinking up some clever accidental death scenario. With an irritated grunt, Han followed Sanderson out into the bustling street.

As Han headed back towards the barrister's chambers, his phone vibrated in his pocket. After dropping back a little further, he accepted the call.

"Nice night for walk?" Gabriel said in a deliberately stilted way.

"Terminator," Han replied, rolling his eyes.

"I spent ages thinking up that one and had to Google it to check," Gabriel said with mild amusement. "There's no tripping you up. It's nice that you're getting plenty of exercise, but you're not exactly achieving much yet."

"Give me a bloody chance. You wanted … *special* circumstances, remember?"

"Oh, yes, I know. Did you read the full file? Maybe I should've highlighted it for you."

Keeping his eyes on the target, Han mentally thumbed through the pages of Sanderson's dossier.

"Extracurricular activities," Gabriel offered helpfully.

Ah so, Han thought to himself. *Sanderson was a bit of a pervert. He liked a bit of the auto-erotic asphyxia shenanigans.* "He does like his oranges," Han said finally.

"You hit the nail on the head."

"Bit clichéd though, isn't it?" Han said, but he was already mulling over his options.

"I would prefer to call it tried and tested," Gabriel replied.

"Oh, I can imagine," Han said. Over the years, so many celebrities and political figures had croaked it through strangling themselves for their kicks. *How many of those cases were really accidental?* he wondered.

"I think you can take it from here," Gabriel said. "Now go and have some fun."

"You too, sweetheart," Han said then ended the call and pocketed the phone. It had happened plenty of times in the past, so it was a simple solution that wouldn't raise too many eyebrows, except from his wife and kids, of course.

His home was out of the question – there were too many comings and goings with his family. He had a receptionist and a secretary at his chambers, but his file did say that he worked late on a regular basis – sometimes with his secretary bent over his desk (there was another unbridled cliché right there), but also sometimes for a little 'alone time'.

Han clapped his hands together then glanced at his watch. Time to put this little show on hold and come back later better prepared.

***

Han returned home and spent the afternoon studying the plans to Sanderson's office building and the buildings either side.

After dinner, Han set off back to Fleet Street. This time, his goody bag also contained an orange, just in case Geoffrey hadn't brought his own.

The building to the right was separated by a narrow lane, but the one to the left, some sort of legal bookshop, was attached.

According to the plans, it had easy access between buildings via the roof.

He had already checked the bookshop's website, so he knew it would still be open.

Inside the shop, half a dozen well-dressed patrons were browsing the shelves. There was a quiet austerity about the place. No one gave Han a second glance and the ageing bow-tied gent manning the till was in a serious discussion with a customer about the forthcoming release of a book on matrimonial law.

Han strode with purpose to the back of the shop where he leafed through some random titles for a few minutes. There was no CCTV, which was a bonus. Once he was sure that no one was paying him any attention, he opened a door marked STAFF ONLY and slipped through into a corridor with storerooms, an office and a kitchenette and toilet leading off. Luckily, no other members of staff were anywhere to be seen. At the far end of the corridor was another door. He opened it and discovered a stairwell and an emergency exit. He ascended five flights of stairs until he finally reached the top floor with an access hatch and fold down ladders.

He carefully checked and discovered that the hatch wasn't alarmed. After slipping out onto the roof, he drew up the ladders and closed the hatch once more.

Staying low, he picked his way across the roof and eased himself over the two-foot lip that separated the two buildings. The access hatch on Sanderson's building was alarmed, but only with a simple sensor strip.

After unzipping his tool pouch, he created a bridge with a strip of copper wire, so that when he opened the hatch the lost connection would not trip the alarm. It was a little fiddly working it into place, but it was covert entry 101 from his tutor at the Consortium training facility.

As he slipped the pouch back into his coat pocket, he smiled. That was the first proper use of his Consortium training. It deserved some sort of fanfare or at least a quick nip of Jack Daniels to celebrate. He settled for a quick pat on the back and then eased inside.

The top floor was deserted and in darkness. The rooms were either empty and disused or just being used as a dumping ground for dusty boxes and old fixtures and furniture.

He made himself comfortable in an office cluttered with old desks, chairs and filing cabinets. He chose the far corner that was hidden from view from a casual observer who might pop their head in through the door.

Reading his Kindle to kill time, he waited another hour for cleaning staff to finish making their rounds and then headed down to Sanderson's third floor office. There would certainly be a security guard and possibly one or two other people working late, so he took his time, pausing to listen every few yards before advancing.

The reception and waiting area of Sanderson's office was deserted, but still lit. A meeting room to one side was in darkness, which left Geoffrey's office. The door was closed, but there was a sliver of light visible beneath it.

Han crept up to the door and listened. He could just make out the tapping of keys, but nothing else. He waited and listened for several minutes, straining to determine whether he was alone or not.

Other than tapping and the occasional creak of an office chair, there was silence. No panting or groaning, so it was safe to say that his secretary wasn't 'working' late with him. *Game time.*

He took a lock knife out of his pocket and opened the door. He strode into the room with knife in hand and pointed the glistening blade at the suited man behind the expansive mahogany desk.

Geoffrey Sanderson was engrossed in the report that he was typing up, so at first did not even look up. It was only when the door shut behind Han that he glanced up, irritated. The look of irritation turned to shock as his eyes fell upon the knife. "Wha—"

Walking over to the desk, Han said, "Mister Sanderson" in his best Agent Smith voice.

Still staring at the knife, Sanderson said, "Er ... I ..." He couldn't decide whether to attempt to lie or not.

"Shut the fuck up and listen. It seems that you've been living two lives, Mister Sanderson. In one, you're the respectable barrister

66

fighting injustice, paying your taxes, fucking your wife occasionally, fucking your secretary … more often."

"How dare you! Just you wait one—"

Han thrust the knife close to Sanderson's face, causing him to shrink away. "Shut the fuck up. I know everything about you. In your other life, you're paid by gangsters and a deluge of lowlifes to beat the judicial system by any and all means necessary. I'd like to say that one of these lives has a future, but in actual fact neither do."

The initial shock had worn off and was rapidly being replaced with terror. "I … I … please, I'm just doing my job."

Han walked around the desk, shaking his head. "The SS guards from Auschwitz tried that shit. It didn't wash at the Nuremberg Trials and it sure isn't gonna wash now."

Indignation briefly suppressed Sanderson's fear. "You're comparing *me* to mass murdering Nazis?"

Han laughed. "I know, crazy, eh?"

"I'm doing a difficult job here … I work within the constraints of the law …"

"You use and abuse the law – there's a big difference."

"I don't make the laws!" Sanderson's voice was shrill with desperation. "It's not my fault that we have an imperfect system."

"I'm sure you tell yourself that over and over again to try to justify what you do," Han said with a sneer.

"There's … got to be …"

"No," Han said, "there isn't. Now, I also happen to know that you like strangling yourself and cumming in your trousers."

Sanderson's bright red face shook and beads of sweat stood out on his forehead.

"No sense trying to deny it. I know *everything* about you."

Tears rolled down the man's face as he uttered, "Who … are … you?"

"I represent the righteous and you, the selfish and tyranny of evil men." Han smiled and produced the orange from his pocket. "And I will lay my vengeance upon you."

Seeing the orange tipped the man over the edge. He tried to scramble out of his chair, clawing away from the intruder, sobbing uncontrollably.

To Han, it was such a wretched display, the man barely registered as human at all, which just made what he was about to do all the easier.

He clicked his tongue with mild irritation and yanked the barrister back into his seat. In a blur of movement, he applied a chokehold around his neck. The man's thrashing struggle was no match for Han's grip. As he maintained the pressure, Han's thoughts turned to his own grumbling stomach.

As Sanderson vainly grasped at Han's arms and face, Han said, "I could really go for an omelette right now. How about you?"

The man's wide streaming eyes stared up at him. *"Please ..."*

"Nearly there, Mr Sanderson," Han said absently.

The barrister's strangled cries quickly subsided to whispered gurgles. His eyes then rolled up into the back of his head and he passed out through lack of oxygen to the brain.

After checking his pulse, Han then took the man's tie off and dragged him over to the door. Rather than risk using his own knife, he rummaged through the desk drawers and found a small kitchen knife and sliced the orange in two, leaving one half on the desk. He then made a rudimentary noose with the tie and attached it to a coat hook on the back of the door. After hauling the barrister up against the door, he slipped the noose around his neck.

Sanderson was beginning to come around, so Han jammed the orange into his mouth then held the man's nose, forcing him to suck in hard.

As Sanderson's wide eyes fixed on his, Han gripped him by the scruff of the neck with one hand while holding the orange in place with the other and then gradually leant back. The tie snapped taut against the man's neck and bit into the skin. The skin quickly changed from angry red to purple.

Han held the man in place as he choked. Just as he started to lose consciousness, he released the pressure. He repeated the process several times.

Han couldn't help but feel a little soiled by the whole experience. He imagined that even under these extreme circumstances Sanderson was probably still getting off on it on some base level. The thought made him cringe, but he had to admit that it would look even more real if the man did actually cream his pants during the procedure. *Christ, Gabriel didn't say getting perverts off would be part of the job description.* Visions of a farmer masturbating his prize bull filled his mind. The images almost made him lose his grip.

Glancing at Sanderson's bloated purple face, he said, "This shit is *nasty*." The barrister's eyes were rolling around like marbles. He doubted that he would even know which way was up right now.

When he could stand it no more, Han kept the pressure on until the man was dead. He checked his pulse then gave the room a once over. Before leaving, he checked the man's pulse one more time, just to be on the safe side.

"Sweet dreams, asshole," he muttered then carefully eased the door open just enough so that he could slide out and then closed it behind him with Geoffrey Sanderson still hanging limply from his blue and red King's College tie. The fear and tension was gone from his features, leaving an almost serene facade.

The bookshop was closed, of course, so Han returned to the top floor office-cum-store room. He unrolled his sleeping bag then pulled out a Tupperware container of sandwiches.

He examined one limp ham and salad triangle and grimaced. An omelette would have gone down far better. At least he had a bag of crisps and a hipflask of whiskey to aid digestion.

He plucked out his Kindle and lay on his makeshift bed, eating, sipping whiskey and losing himself in the world of Douglas Adams.

Early the next morning, Han made his way up to the roof and waited. He kept an eye on the street below until he knew the bookshop to be busy. Then he headed downstairs and slipped back into the shop, where he took his time, browsing several sections, before heading home.

As he walked into his apartment, his phone rang. Han knew instinctively who it would be. "Hi, Gabe."

"Well done," Gabriel said in earnest. "Perfectly executed and a creative entry and exit. Top marks."

"Thanks," Han said as he poured himself a shot of Jack. He hadn't managed to get much sleep on the concrete floor, so with fatigue creeping into every joint, he shuffled over to the sofa and dropped into its loving embrace.

"You must be exhausted," Gabriel was saying. "Get some R&R. You've earned it."

"You're too kind," Han said dreamily.

Han sat there for some time after he had said his goodbyes, staring at the magnolia wall, his shot of whiskey untouched. An image of his old bedroom, its walls not dissimilar, sprung to mind. It was lacking the vast array of movie memorabilia, of course, but it struck him nonetheless.

A stray shard of morning sunlight poked through the gap in the curtains. Was that a faint smell of dog lingering just beyond his senses? *Jumanji*. No matter how often he would wash the sheets and hose the place down with air freshener, he could never quite eliminate that hint of canine. God, how he missed it.

He knocked back the whiskey then curled up on the sofa and drifted into a listless sleep.

This is no dream! This is really happening!

CHAPTER 6

Lionheart was restless. He wandered the city centre backstreets of Glasgow, his mood relentlessly darkening in unison with the sky. He had been waiting for a sign for far too long.

It had been months since executing the Saracen couple in their home and the cause beckoned. Although satisfying on one level, his last assignment had been a rather artless time-sensitive kill, so had lacked the preparation that some of his more elaborate set pieces demanded. The gratification was not only in the kill itself – that was all too fleeting – it was also in the delicate planning of every minuscule and delicious detail.

In between assignments, he liked to travel around the country, observing his countrymen and the Saracen parasites who lurked amongst them. In some places those scum outnumbered his brethren. It was soul-destroying to witness, but it was necessary. He had to continuously remind himself of the validity of the cause and of the problems that he had to solve. They bled the nation dry whilst corrupting the nation's purity.

Some would argue that the gene pool had been continuously corrupted throughout history, pre-dating even the Romans, and that the people of Britain were and had always been a melting pot of ethnic diversity. His answer was simple – they were invaders and some were repelled and some were not, but all were fought. Although far more insidious, this was still just a foreign invasion.

Increasing racial tensions between rival white and Asian gangs in Glasgow had hit the national press, so he had travelled north to see for himself.

The fucking Saracens were now attacking the good people of Glasgow. The war was spreading daily. And still no damn sign. Well, if they would not send out the call, he would just take up the sword again regardless. He was tired of waiting. He would either get a slap on the wrist or be executed. It didn't matter to him either way. He was ready to die for the cause.

It was early evening and Sauchiehall Street was already lively with drunken revellers. It was payday, so it was going to get messy. Lionheart shook his head and let out a deep sigh. This pervasive immorality was happening in every city in Great Britain.

Most of the ignorant masses had no idea and no care about the cause or the war that raged around them. They cared for nothing, but pleasures of the flesh. He was by no means a priest – he liked a drink and he also liked to bed a woman every now and then. He could not bring himself to become attached to one, and he certainly did not have the time or inclination to woo one, so he preferred to pay for a woman's time. It was far easier to pay for a quick fuck. He had nothing against prostitutes – they were performing a valuable service to society. Without them, more men would turn to rape. It was one thing to rape the wives of your enemy – that was a soldier's God given right. It was part of the spoils of war to plant your seed into the womb of the enemy and also necessary to pervert their gene pool. But to rape an innocent – that was eternal damnation for the soul.

An image flickered behind his intense eyes caused a brief grimace. *A bedroom, late at night. Hiding beneath the covers, a creak as the door slowly opened …*

An argument outside a Wetherspoon's pub up ahead drew his attention. Three Asian youths were in a dispute with a white man and his girlfriend. *Probably trying to provoke him into a fight by insulting his woman*, he thought as he closed the distance.

He heard sirens that could only be a street or two away. He didn't have much time. Keeping his hand in his pocket, he grasped the hypodermic and, using thumb and forefinger, eased the protective sheath off. The syringe contained three times the lethal dosage of sodium thiopental, so would be more than sufficient.

He drew it out of his pocket as he reached within a couple of yards of the closest Saracen. Then, as the group continued to hurl obscenities at each other, he jabbed one youth in the arm, pressed the plunger all the way and continued to walk away at speed, the syringe still in his hand. It all happened in three seconds.

The youth cried out in a delayed reaction, most likely due to alcohol. He grabbed his arm, shouting, "What the fuck, man?" He turned to look around him, but several people were walking past in both directions. "Who the fuck did that, yae bastard?"

"What's up, Daz?" his friend asked, taking his attention off the racist yob they had been arguing with for the past five minutes.

"I … I think someone stabbed us, eh …" The youth suddenly bent over double and his legs gave out. He fell to the ground, his body wracked with violent spasms.

Everyone fell silent and stared at the convulsing man as he began foaming at the mouth.

"Daz? Fuck!" his friend cried out, dropping to his knees to help his stricken friend. Glancing up at the third youth, he yelled, "Call an ambulance!"

Lionheart took a narrow side street onto Sauchiehall Lane, casting the empty syringe into a skip as he walked by. As he headed for Bath Street, a police car sped past.

A smile touched his lips and he let out a satisfied sigh. With each step, his rising bloodlust dissipated, leaving him calm and satisfied once more.

It was another hasty and unimaginative kill, but it served its purpose, like a field dressing in the absence of a surgical team. It was another casualty for the Saracens. In the end, that was all that mattered.

Still, he did long for something delightfully sophisticated to sink his teeth into. Soon.

A VW Beetle pulled into the street of terraced houses. Cara parked outside her flat and stepped out into the cold dawn air. The sun was still just below the horizon, leaving the street bathed in a listless grey. She reached back into the car to retrieve her shoulder bag then locked up. As she turned to her flat, a noise caught her attention.

She glanced around, frowning. The street was deserted, as you would expect at such an ungodly hour. There was not a single light on in the street yet. She then noticed that the streetlights were not on either. It also occurred to her that her Beetle was the only car in the street. Normally the street would be full of parked cars at this time of the morning.

A shiver ran between her shoulder blades. Berating herself under her breath, she shrugged off the ominous sensation and headed for her front door.

As she approached the door, she stopped dead, a gasp caught on her lips. The poor half-light had disguised the markings until she was only a couple of feet away. In what might have been charcoal, a large black cross had been drawn on the door with RIP CARA written across the centre.

A twig snapped like the crack of a rifle shot.

Cara spun around. "Who's there? Who did this?" she demanded, her police training managing to conceal some of her rising fear. The street was still devoid of life. She strained her ears, listening for any sound of movement. Nothing. Not even a breeze to rustle next door's conifers.

She turned back to the door to find a figure looming in front of her, eyes glowing like fire. She instinctively raised her hands as the figure surged towards her, mouth opening to reveal extended yellow canines in a soundless snarl.

Han snapped awake, gasping and blinking in the darkness. He sat up and fumbled in the darkness for his phone. Illuminating the screen, he saw that it was after ten in the evening. He had slept through the entire day.

The image of Cara's terrified face burned in his mind's eye. He realised that his hand was instinctively searching for Jumanji under the duvet. He withdrew it instantly and stared at his fingertips for a time.

The darkness seemed to bear down on him. He turned on his bedside lamp and his heavy breathing gradually began to subside. He rubbed his face then padded into the kitchen. The open bottle of *Old No. 7* was on the bench where he left it. Despite a headache from dehydration, he poured himself a shot and knocked it back. The heat sliding down into his belly did nothing for his headache, but it did go a small way to gathering his senses.

Rubbing his temples, he remembered waking up on the sofa with an aching neck and no idea of the time. With eyes still half shut, he had shuffled into the bedroom and promptly collapsed.

The Sanderson gig had clearly taken more out of him than he had first realised and he was not talking about the pseudo sexual element.

He was Han Whitman, a legend in his own lifetime. Of course, not that many people knew that he was still in his own lifetime, but that was not the point. He wasn't prone to blowing his own trumpet anyway, but he was the man who managed to wipe out an entire village and a prison full of Her Majesty's nastiest. Was he getting old or was it all the injuries that he had sustained in recent years? He had taken more than his fair share of knocks along the way that was for sure, and the big 40 was approaching quicker than Wolf-Biederman. Still, a little voice uttered, *It's not the years, it's the mileage ...*

It was his first assignment – call a spade a spade – his first assassination. He had nearly died and spent several months recuperating and training. The first one was bound to be tough.

He shook his head and shoulders in a physical attempt to dispel the lingering fatigue then knocked back another shot of whiskey. He slowly began to feel human once more. "Am I human?" he asked the bottle. "Or am I dancer? Or is it denser?" Han snorted in the darkness. "Stupid bloody lyric either way."

Gabriel had told him to get some rest and recuperation, so maybe he should do just that. Maybe a little road trip was the answer. Gabriel would not be happy about it, but he probably wouldn't be all that surprised either.

***

The drive up to Leeds was uneventful, but his impatience made it a frustrating one. Han's thoughts were consumed with Cara and, the closer he got, the more nervous he became. He tried shuffling through every scrap of music on his iPhone and every music station, but nothing managed to sooth his unsettled mood. Nothing could distract him, not for a second. He had to keep forcing his foot off the accelerator to keep the rented car under eighty miles per hour.

As he pulled into Cara's street, his phone rang. It caused a brief twinge, but Han guessed who it would be. He was surprised that it had taken him so long to call. "Hi, Gabe."

"You do realise that this is not a good idea, don't you?" Gabriel said, skipping niceties. "In fact, in the history of bad ideas, this ranks up there with the worst of them."

"I know," Han said.

"Your first assignment went very well. It would be a shame to undo that good work."

"I know," Han repeated. With a sigh, he added, "I'd like to say I'm sorry about it, but I'm not. It's just something I have to do."

"I don't have to remind you of the rules or your obligation."

"No, you don't."

Gabriel hung up. Han tossed the phone aside and pulled up on the opposite side of the street a few doors away from Cara's flat.

An old woman in a wide-brimmed floppy hat shuffled by, dragging a scraggy and ancient-looking Yorkshire Terrier. As they drew parallel, the old dog squinted up at him and offered a squeaky growl. The old woman glowered at him and then said, "Come along, Monty. Leave the strange man be."

Han stared after them, shaking his head. Prepared for a long wait, he picked up a thermos flask from the passenger footwell and poured himself a drink. As he sipped coffee, he opened up his

Kindle and started to read, glancing up over the top of the device every few minutes.

Cara didn't show until lunchtime. Han was biting into a cheese sandwich when her car parked up outside the flat. As she got out, the first thing Han noticed was that she had let her hair grow longer; her blonde locks were lapping at her shoulders. The second thing he become aware of as she stepped into view from behind the car was the unmistakable bulge that her jacket strained to cover.

Han spat a chunk of bread onto the dashboard. "My God," he managed, his wide staring eyes blinking at the sight of his heavily pregnant former girlfriend. She appeared to be ready to drop at any moment and was struggling with several carrier bags.

He managed to resist an almost overwhelming urge to rush to her aid. That compulsion acutely reminded him of the first time they met. It had been outside the Adelphi in Leeds, where an argument had turned into a full-scale street brawl. At the time, he had thought that he was just going to the aid of a couple of coppers out of their depth. He waded through the chavs, including one charming Vicky Pollard type, spitting and hissing, *Yer better back the fuck off unless you want some, you cunt.* They had been like a pack of rabid dogs and one of those unfortunate officers had turned out to be Cara. He still remembered seeing the splash of blonde hair, her upturned blue eyes and the graze on her cheek.

He had to swallow to quell the lump in his throat. His mind automatically calculated the time they had been apart, despite cursing himself for it. Eight months. Cara was pregnant with his child. She probably hadn't even found out herself when he had gone on that fateful trip to Dorset.

She was going to have his baby. It had to be his. *He was going to be a father!*

Cara glanced over. Han froze, but then he realised that she was looking above him into the sky. She had a wistful expression and, even from a distance, Han could see the bruising around her eyes. Then, she turned and struggled up the short path and disappeared inside.

Han stared at the door long after it closed, feeling utterly lost. There had been a fleeting moment when he had wanted to shriek with joy. But then he had made out Cara's forlorn features and had realised the brutal reality. He was dead to Cara and dead to his own unborn child. He could never know them, not as who he was or who he had become. His brief joy turned to misery.

He held his head in his hands and wept.

As the tears dried, his phone rang. Wiping his face, he accepted the call.

"I'm sorry, Han," Gabriel said. "I tried to shield you …"

Han heard genuine sorrow in Gabriel's voice. He was a curious breed indeed. He was quite happy to send deranged psychopaths on murderous errands, but deep down, he seemed like such a gentle soul. "Thanks, Gabe," he heard himself say. "I … I had no idea."

"No, I know. She had no idea herself until two weeks after. She has good friends and her family around her. And Jumanji."

"Yeah." His voice sounded distant, disembodied. At least they've got each other …

"Take care, Han," Gabriel was saying.

Han cleared his throat and managed a feeble goodbye.

The phone dropped from his hand into his lap. He gripped the steering wheel and pressed his forehead against it, clenching his jaw. One thought carved its way through the anguish. *I could've had a life and a family with Cara. It was all snatched away by …*

***

Han spent the next few days at the Chevin Country Park Hotel and Spa in Otley while he made the necessary enquiries. It was surprisingly easy. Relentlessly, his waking hours as well as his dreams were tormented with thoughts of Cara and his unborn child; what could have been … what should have been.

Of course, Gabriel got wind of his plans, but, as with Cara, he just offered a polite warning and then stepped back.

***

78

The room was in darkness. A woman slept soundlessly in bed, only the merest whisper of her breathing evidence that she was alive at all.

A figure stepped out of the shadows, looming over the sleeping form. He stood, watching. The silence enveloped him, consumed him as seconds turned into minutes.

The woman moaned softly and turned over, her face falling into view. Carol Belmont moaned a second time then settled once more.

Han continued to watch her, studying her features. This was the woman who stole his life with Cara and destroyed a chance at happiness with a family of his own. In one fleeting second, with the squeeze of a trigger, she changed everything and his old life ended.

Her eyes twitched under their closed lids. He wondered whether she was she reliving their past encounters or, with his believed demise, had she finally managed to find some semblance of peace? Was this woman damaged beyond repair or gradually healing?

She had been through a great deal and Haydon had only been the start. She had genuinely cared for Detective Wright's son. Maybe she had hoped against hope that they could have had a normal life together too ...

The longer he stood captivated with the sleeping woman, the more his burning anger ebbed away, leaving only a cold weariness. Then quite unexpectedly, a truth struck him. It was so definite and powerful that he had to take an unsteady step backwards. His hand clasped his mouth to stifle a sob.

Carol moaned once more, but did not move.

Han's arm fell to his side as he stared open-mouthed at her. The truth was simple and obvious; Carol was not to blame for anything, she was completely innocent. Right from the very start, she had just been a victim unwillingly dragged from one terrible circumstance to the next. He had chosen to embark on the experiment with Haydon, thereby setting into motion the entire chain of events that led to their confrontation in the lockup garage and ultimately brought him to the point where he now stood. There was no one to blame except himself.

He was a big boy. It was about fucking time that he took responsibility for his actions. Of course, that also meant that he was at least in part responsible for both his mum's and Perry's deaths as well. His dad may have physically killed them, but he was just as much to blame as Charlie. If he had not have embarked upon the experiment they would both be still alive. Charlie's manipulation would have amounted to sod all if he had not acted upon it.

He hung his head and closed his eyes. He remained there for some time, the darkness engulfing him and the silence bearing witness.

Finally, he slipping back out the way he had entered, leaving Carol sleeping and blissfully unaware of the intrusion.

As Han drove south through the night, back to his new life, his phone rang. He knew who it would be, but he felt drained and tired, so the company – any company – would be better than being alone with his own thoughts and regrets.

He accepted the call. "Hi, Gabe."

"Hi, Han," Gabriel replied, his tone jovial. "I hope you're hands free. Safety first, you know?"

Han shook his head and managed a washed out smile. "You know me, I'm always careful."

"Well, not always …"

"Fair point."

"Do you feel better after your late night visit? Did it have the desired cathartic effect?"

"That wasn't my original intention," Han said as he stared ahead at the near deserted M1 stretching out ahead of him.

"I know and I don't mind saying that I'm relieved that you didn't embark on the path that you were originally planning." Gabriel paused for a moment then added, "So, how do you feel?"

Han bit back the urge for a sarcastic response, instead, saying, "Tired. Home truths tend to be somewhat draining." As an afterthought, he added, "Don't worry, I haven't discovered a newfound respect for life or anything. I just no longer blame Carol Belmont for anything."

"You are a deeply complex person, Han," Gabriel said without humour. "You're not like the others, and I mean that as the highest compliment."

"I'm no different."

"You are – the others have a predictability about them, even when they're being unpredictable. We know precisely how they tick and how to manipulate and control them. We understand their thought processes and their moral compasses, regardless of how skewed they are. If it had been anyone else, we would have intervened before you reached Carol Belmont. We would not have taken the risk. But, I knew you were different ... changed."

"Why are you telling me this?"

There was silence for a time and Han stared out at the open road, lost in his thoughts. He opened his mouth to ask whether Gabriel was still on the other end of the phone, but then his handler finally spoke. "This may sound like I'm over simplifying things here a bit – and I suppose I am – but, the main reason is that you're actually not a bad person."

Han raised his eyebrows and let out an involuntary snort. "You're kidding, right? After everything I've done?"

"No, don't get me wrong, you've done some bad things – horrendous things – but haven't you stopped to think about Phase Two of the experiment? Not just in the planning, but really stopped to analyse it? With that, on some level, you were searching for redemption, weren't you?"

"Closure," Han lied. "There's a difference."

"I'm sure closure was one part of it, but certainly not all of it. And that's not even mentioning the fact that your father spent most of your life manipulating you in the most cruel and sadistic manner. When all's said and done, you're a decent person who's done some very bad things."

"What does that even mean?"

Gabriel sighed. "I don't know, forget I mentioned it. I'm just glad you did the right thing tonight. That woman has been through enough. Drive carefully and we'll talk soon, alright?"

Han said goodbye and ended the call, but his mind could not shake the conversation and Gabriel's comments. *Aye, that Han Whitman, he's a decent enough bloke. Sure, he's made some mistakes – murdered a few hundred people in cold blood – but does that make him a bad man? Everyone makes mistakes, right? Who hasn't butchered the occasional innocent, eh? He's only human after all.*

He tried to force a laugh, but it came out as a strangled cough. Could a person who had committed such atrocities possibly find redemption? Could he ever be deserving of it? He had murdered *children*, for Christ's sake. *Haley* ... Surely *the* ultimate sin. It had all been part of the experiment, but he damn well knew at the time that it was terribly wrong, but he did it anyway, for the sake of the experiment.

The feelings of his first kill flooded back to him. The image of him straddling beautiful young Mandy Foster filled his mind's eye. She was splayed out on the sodden forest floor as he stabbed her over and over again. He remembered sneering, slicing, penetrating that young porcelain flesh. He remembered the glimpse of her exposed breast. Then the tears, the sobbing, all the while the rain washing the blood from her pale face and staining the mud. Her lifeless eyes, staring, accusing.

Had he been just fooling himself with the entire basis of Phase Two? Surely it had just been self-serving and ridiculous from the start. *Here's an idea, Han, old buddy, as you're not feeling too peachy about the slaughter of so many innocents, why don't you trot off and slaughter a load of bad guys to balance up the books. Oh, yes, of course! The experiment isn't finished. This is the sequel!* It had all been a thinly veiled guise from the very start.

Han wiped the tears from his face and, through a clenched jaw, muttered, "What a load of bollocks." The bitter words were lost amidst the drone of the engine.

Driving south on the A1, he noticed the next turnoff was for Cramlington and Seaton Burn. Without thinking, he yanked the steering wheel to the left and took the turnoff, tyres screeching their displeasure. He drove through the darkened streets of Seaton Burn before reaching the small mining village that now consumed his thoughts.

The car slowed to a crawl. There were no lights on in the village. The old semi detached council houses appeared bereft of any life, quiet, foreboding. The darkness pressed in from all sides, making Han feel squashed and claustrophobic. He stopped the car at the end of the street and stared at his mother's house.

It looked exactly the same as his last visit over a year ago. He had no idea whether it was even still in the family. Would Karl have been able to bring himself to sell it? Doubtful. There was no car in the drive and all the curtains were still open. It did not appear to be occupied and there were no estate agent signs nailed to the brickwork. His childhood home, like a lot of things, was in limbo.

He got out of the car and walked up to the house in silence. After a quick glance over his shoulder, he picked the lock on the front door and slipped inside.

The first thing to strike him was the smell. There was a hint of foist, but the predominant smell was as he always remembered it. It was a mixture of polish, old wood and a hint of cigarette smoke and it smelt just like home.

He held his head in his hands and wept quietly for several minutes.

After composing himself, he drifted from room to room through the house. All his mum's personal possessions had been removed, but the furniture remained. Mum's bedroom was the only room that had dramatically changed. It was empty and had been completely redecorated.

The emergency services had responded in record time – quick enough to extinguish the fire before it spread beyond the bedroom, but not quick enough to save his mum. Charlie had made damn sure of that.

He stood there for a time, staring at the blank walls. It had been redecorated months earlier, but he could still detect the faint aroma of fresh paint. Lurking beneath it, there was also the merest suggestion of smoke.

Swinging the door open, the boys cascaded into the bedroom, arms clutching bulging Christmas stockings.

"It's Christmas!" they were chanting as they dove onto the bed.

Mum dragged the covers from her face, her bruised eyes betraying an acute lack of sleep. Despite her crippling fatigue from working double shifts in the pub and juggling Christmas preparations, she beamed and sat up, wiping long strands of red hair from her face.

"Merry Christmas, boys." She snatched a lighter and packet of cigarettes from the bedside cabinet and lit up. "Let's see what Father Christmas has brought you then."

Han stared at bare floor where her bed used to be. There was no physical trace of it or of his mum, but he could still see her there. Exhausted and stressed with money worries, but smiling and full of love. With indescribable reluctance, he turned away and left the room forever.

He stood with his hand on the front door handle and turned back one final time. Scarcely above a whisper, he said, "Goodbye, mum. I'm sorry."

He drove back to London in reflective silence.

***

The small hospital room was bathed in darkness, apart from a couple of low wattage night-lights. Cara lay in the only bed, staring up at the ceiling and concentrating on her breathing. The contractions were coming in knotted waves every ten minutes and, as another gripped her for almost a minute, she sucked in a deep breath and closed her eyes.

As the pain coursed through her abdomen and lower back, her thoughts turned to the father of her unborn child. He was a psychopathic serial killer and pathological liar. Nevertheless, despite all the horrific things he had done, it didn't change the fact that she did still love him. She hated him too, in equal measure, but one could never quite extinguish the other. She wished that she could just hold his hand and hear his reassuring voice tell her that it would be okay. And for that she also hated herself. How could she be so weak?

As the contraction eased, she suddenly felt a new, sharper pain. It was so acute that her entire body jerked in a violent spasm. She gripped her swollen belly, whimpering.

Something was wrong. She fumbled in the gloom for the nurse call button. As she pressed it, another stab of pain caused her to cry out. "Nurse!"

A nurse arrived moments later, switching the main lights on as she entered.

"How are you doing, sweetie?" the older woman asked as she moved to the bedside.

The pain wracked Cara's entire body and this time she screamed. "God, help me!"

The nurse's initial motherly concern turned to alarm. Pulling the covers from her, she gasped and stepped back, a hand instinctively covering her mouth.

The white sheet was awash with blood. It was thick, coagulated and oozing over the sides of the bed. It hit the polished floor with a wet slap and began pooling at the nurse's feet. As she called for assistance, Cara screamed again, tears running down her contorted face as she begged for help.

As the nurse reached out to put a comforting hand on the agonised woman there was a loud crack. Her hand stopped in mid air and she stared at the pregnant woman's gown. Her swollen belly jerked upwards and a dark stain spread across the pink material. Cara's screams were abruptly silenced. Then something tore through the blood-stained material, something razor-sharp and dripping blood and jelly-like placenta.

The nurse staggered back, horrified, as a creature emerged from the gaping wound. It was a human baby, but it turned to face the nurse and emitted a venomous hiss through needle-like teeth. With fingers like vicious elongated talons, it beseeched the horrified nurse.

Then, with a ravenous shriek, the creature tore free from its dead mother and leapt at the screaming nurse.

Han snapped awake, screaming, "Holy-mother-fucking-shit!"

He was bathed in sweat with his heart pounding. He sat up, clutching his chest and glanced around the bedroom. No Krueger-like offspring was waiting to pounce from the shadows. No Alien half-breed lurked under the bed. He was alone, in the dark.

As his senses returned and his gasping breaths died down, he sat back and said aloud, "What the fuck is the matter with me?" It was a rhetorical question.

Dude, where's my dojo?

CHAPTER 7

A couple of weeks passed by without any news from Gabriel or the Troy Consortium. Han did little, except eat, sleep and train. Cara played on his mind constantly, wondering how she was and whether she given birth to their baby. Such thoughts only provoked further intense exercise. He joined the local amateur mixed martial arts club and a local rock-climbing wall. Anything to keep his mind occupied.

He hadn't climbed for several years, so started on the easier bouldering routes before gradually progressing up to the tougher grades. He preferred free climbing for its lack of restrictions and isolation. It was just him against the wall. He did switch to ropes from time to time, but that was more for necessity than desire. When an appropriate ballast bag wasn't available he had to rely on a belay partner and that stole some of his enjoyment.

In contrast, he allowed himself a little more social interaction at the MMA club. The rest of the members were way out of his league, but, for a time, he managed to play down his skills. The instruction in Brazilian Jiu Jitsu, Thai Boxing and regular boxing wasn't bad, but they weren't at the same level as Amwolf and the other Consortium trainers. It was, however, one of the MMA instructors who finally clocked him.

His Thai Boxing instructor was a wiry man in his late twenties with a skinhead and a face that had taken way too many hits over the years. Diego Petley had Mediterranean blood, but spoke like an East End gangster.

After an intensive one on one session, Diego cast aside the towel that he had been using to wipe the sweat and blood from his face. As he picked up a bottle of water, he said, "So, what's the fucking story here, mate?"

A trickle of blood dribbled down the side of Han's face from a cut above his eye. He was breathing harder than he needed to, but then stopped and stared at the instructor. "What do you mean?" Han asked finally.

Diego was watching him out of the corner of his eye as he gulped down some water. After casting the bottle into his bag, he folded his arms and said, "With you. You're holding back – you're a lot better than you're making out. Why hold back and why the con? Are you taking me for a mug?" A flash of anger behind the younger man's probing eyes.

Han changed into a clean t-shirt, depicting Jeff Bridges with the quote, *El Duderino, if you're not into the whole brevity thing*. He stared at Diego for a moment and then shrugged. "I didn't want to be the new kid showing off, that's all. I'm also a little out of practice, so I just thought I'd ease myself back into it."

Diego continued to study him, weighing him up. It was all feasible, but it just didn't quite sit right. "I ain't happy about someone sparring with people who are at a much lower level. It ain't fucking done. Not in my gaff."

"I'm sorry. I guess I didn't see it from that point of view."

They locked eye contact, but then Diego shrugged and said, "No harm done – you weren't taking the piss or nothing. Just a little ... misguided, eh?" He offered his hand and Han shook it. "Next week there's no bullshit. I'll put you in with the best I've got and we'll take it from there."

Diego was true to his word. The following week, he fielded two different fighters against Han, one bigger and stronger, the second fast and agile. This time Han did not hold back. The rest of the class stopped sparring to watch. They both put up a good fight, but they were no match for Han.

After the applause and chatter had died down, Diego invited Han out for a beer.

"Cheers," Han said and sipped his pint of Guinness.

Diego left his bottle untouched, staring at Han. "You're fucking good, mate. How come I ain't heard of you on the circuit before? You could be out there winning silverware, I shit you not."

"I never bothered to go into competition. I wasn't interested in that sort of thing."

"A bloke with your skills not *bothering* to go into competition? That's fucking mental, man. You've got a gift."

Han took another drink as Diego shook his head in disbelief. "So, why did you bother getting so fucking proficient then? If you don't mind me asking."

"Long story."

"I ain't going anywhere and I'm fucking buying. I want to know."

"You've probably heard similar stories before," Han said. "Bit of trouble as a kid. I never seemed to be able to keep my mouth shut, so I used to get into bother a lot. So, I took up karate and boxing from a young age and then did a two stretch in the Army, followed by a stint in close protection. I've always fought in one way or another." Well, most of that was pretty close to the truth, as the best lies always are.

"Squaddie, eh? I was in 2 Para. You?"

"RMP," Han said without missing a beat.

Diego laughed. "Fucking Army copper?"

"That was how I ended up in the close protection game."

"A mate of mine does that stuff – was in 2 Para with me and used to do the doors – big fucker. He's always got a story to tell about hot big-titted celebs, mountains of coke – that sort of shit."

Han shook his head and took another drink of his pint. "Nah, it's not really like that, or at least not for me, it wasn't. It was mostly boring day to day stuff; babysitting businessmen, foreign dignitaries and that sort of thing."

Diego nodded at Han's hand and said, "Lose the fingers in the line of duty?"

"Funnily enough, no. I never got injured on duty. My hand, face and knee were from a car accident."

Diego snorted. "Unlucky, mate."

"I was lucky to make it out alive." *That's the God damn truth!*

"Given what must've been one nasty fucking accident, you seemed to have bounced back alright." Diego fell silent for a moment, a meditative gaze clouding usually bright, dynamic eyes. He shook his head to dispel it and added, "Some blokes don't make it back from that sort of shit … not fully anyway."

Han noted the change in mood, but didn't comment. Instead, he said, "I was lucky – I got some excellent private medical care from my previous employer. I had some amazing people looking after me. They saved my life. And those physios were borderline psychotic."

Diego smiled. "They're all like that, mate." Switching the subject, he asked, "So, what does a battle scarred hard as nails ex-squaddie and ex-bodyguard do for a living these days?"

"You probably wouldn't believe me."

"Try me."

"I'm a writer – I have a movie review column in the Evening Standard."

Diego nearly spat a mouthful of lager across the table. Coughing, he said, "You've got to be shitting me?"

"I'm serious. As well as fighting, my other love has always been movies."

Diego sat back, shaking his head. "You're one interesting motherfucker."

You don't know the half of it! "I'll take that as a compliment."

"Good – it was meant as one."

***

Han got to know Diego better over the following weeks and found him to be a refreshing distraction to the Consortium and thoughts of Cara and their child.

A few drinks after each weekly session turned into a regular occurrence. The training sessions were good, but for Han, the banter over a couple of drinks afterwards became something more to look forward to.

The ex-para turned out to have a wicked sense of humour, but he had depths that even Han was surprised at. The man had turned to Buddhism after the death of his pregnant girlfriend years earlier while he had been involved with Operation Telic in Iraq. By his own admission, he wasn't always one hundred percent devote, the occasional drink being his main vice, but it was a faith that he held very dear. As well as an MMA instructor and competitor, he was also a gifted traceur of the freerunning art of parkour and had also provided some stunt co-ordinator expertise to a couple of Hollywood films.

After another enlightening and entertaining session with Diego, Han headed back to his apartment.

A contentment had settled over him that he had not been acquainted with for quite some time. He could not quite call it happiness, but it made a pleasant change and was certainly a distraction from other thoughts.

It was more perceptible when he was with Diego or spending time climbing or training. However, whenever he was alone for too long, the darker thoughts would creep back in and his mood would darken with them.

As he walked through the dark near deserted streets, those thoughts inevitably leached back to the forefront of his mind.

By the time Han reached his apartment, the fleeting positivity had evaporated, leaving him brooding.

As soon as he opened the door, he knew something was amiss. The hallway light was on and he was certain that he had turned it off before leaving earlier.

He stood motionless, listening. There was silence, apart from the soft hum from the condensing boiler. He edged forward, carefully avoiding the area in front of the door that he knew made a creak when stepped on. As he moved, he slipped his front door key in between his balled up fingers as a makeshift weapon.

In the doorway to the living room, he noticed a figure sitting in the darkness, a glass in hand.

Han flicked the light switch then breathed a sigh of relief. "Help yourself to my whiskey," he said, shaking his head and dropping his keys back into his pocket.

"Thank you," Gabriel said, "I didn't think you would mind."

As Han retrieved the bottle of Jack and a glass from the kitchen, he asked, "To what do I owe this pleasure?"

Gabriel sipped at his whiskey then said, "I've brought you your next assignment."

"No couriers available?" Han topped up Gabriel's glass and then filled his own, before dropping onto the sofa.

"Plenty, but I happened to be in the area and wanted to see you personally."

"That sounds ominous."

Gabriel shook his head. "No, not at all. You've been out on your own for a while now and I know the transition hasn't been easy, so I just thought I'd check in on you."

Han knocked back some whiskey then said, "Thanks, but you don't need to worry about me. I'm fine."

"Well, I'm glad you're settling in. It's great that you're making new friends too."

Han sat forward. "Is that what this is about? Are you worried I might spill the beans?"

"No, not at all, Han," Gabriel said, waving his whiskey glass. "There was no double meaning there. I am happy that you're making friends. You've had a lot to deal with, so a friendly ear, even one that you can't be entirely truthful with, is a lot better than nothing."

Han took another sip of whiskey and then said, "Okay then. But there's something else." He sat back, studying the man. "So what is it then?"

Gabriel did not answer for a time, instead choosing to inspect his glass.

Han hadn't seen him like this before. He appeared troubled, unsure.

Eventually, Gabriel said, "I'm not just your handler, Han. I'd like you to think of me as a friend as well – a confidant; someone who you *can* always be truly honest with. I will always be honest with you."

Han snorted and said, "Aye, right."

"Oh, don't misunderstand, I can't always divulge all the details to you, but everything that I am allowed to tell you, I will. I'll always be straight down the line and no bullshit with you."

Han shrugged. "Fair enough, but why are you telling me this?"

He seemed to struggle with the right words, but he settled with, "I'm not really sure … yet, but as soon as I understand more I will tell you."

"Smoke and mirrors," Han said and added a theatrical wave of his hands, followed by a "*Poof!*"

Gabriel let out a sigh that sounded even more weary than the man looked. "I'm sorry, I don't mean to be vague. As soon as I know more I will explain all – I just wanted to make sure you know that I'm on your side in this."

"Won't your superiors disapprove of a conversation like this?"

"Yes, but it is standard procedure for handlers to use scramblers whenever consulting with operatives, regardless of how secure the location may or may not be, so this conversation is strictly just between the two of us."

***

Long after Gabriel had left, Han sat finishing off the bottle of whiskey and mulling over his handler's words.

Was Gabriel just worried that he might go off the rails like his father had, or was something else going on that he wasn't aware of yet? The whole cloak and dagger act might have all just been a clever psychological trick to keep him onside. Then again …

Unanswered questions kept rattling around inside his head and, despite all the whiskey and the late hour, he felt no urge to retreat to his bed. So, instead, he opened up the dossier and started to thumb through the contents.

This week's lucky contestant is … Greg Rifkin. On the surface, Greg was a family man and local businessman, but he was also a paramilitary commander for a radical breakaway arm of the British National Party, who were responsible for stirring up racial hatred during the recent London riots.

His gangs of thugs had carried out dozens of rapes and assaults on ethnic minorities UK wide. Last week, they had committed their first murder of a young Asian youth in Bristol.

Rifkin was in his fifties, but still had a solid build from his days working on the doors in South London. His life running both a building contractors and a taxi firm had taken him to the more salubrious surroundings of a ten bedroom detached house in Oxford. This sort of thing wouldn't have been allowed to happen in Inspector Morse's day.

Han continued to familiarise himself with Greg Rifkin until the first rays of sun were peeking through the blinds. Massaging his neck, he reluctantly retired to bed, musing that he would have to pick up a new bottle of Jack tomorrow.

***

The next day, with a bit of a sore head, Han began making plans for the Rifkin job.

He lived with his wife and two teenage daughters, so his home would be less than ideal, but it had been stipulated in the dossier that it should be made to look like a botched burglary. That made things tricky. He did not want to risk any innocent bystanders, so he needed to separate Greg from the rest of his family somehow, without raising any suspicions and without putting his family in any unnecessary danger.

His recently discovered respect for innocent life did cause a few additional headaches. It was a little irritating, but he would just have to cope with it.

The family's daily habits were erratic, but the dossier did reveal that his wife attended a zumba class on Thursday nights and the eldest daughter often tagged along. The youngest daughter also spent a lot of time over at a friend's house, so Thursday night became the most viable option.

***

After checking that there was no CCTV in the street, Han parked up a discreet distance away from Rifkin's not unimpressive mansion. The rural street was lined with mature oak trees and each imposing regal property was a unique design to the next. They were all set in large gardens with high fences or walls separating them.

He watched Rifkin's wife come and go. She was attractive, in a big blonde hair and fake tits sort of way. He also observed one daughter and then the next arrive home. The older daughter was the spitting image of her mother – even down to the false tits. The younger one was clearly the black sheep – black hair, hoodie, glasses and head down; she was dripping with emo angst.

Then it was daddy's turn to come home. He pulled up in a white Range Rover and jumped out, all leather jacket and mobile phone surgically attached to his ear. With his solid frame and salt and pepper hair, he resembled Dog from Lock, Stock and Two Smoking Barrels. *Christ, this twat was a fucking walking cliché of a gangster wannabe.* This was going to be more fun than he first thought.

Two cronies turned up an hour later. They were archetypical hard men and, knowing what he knew about Greg Rifkin, entirely predictable. *Hmm, they did make things a little bit more awkward though.* No opportunist robber would normally take on three blokes, let alone *these* three.

A short while later, mum and clone daughter left, followed shortly afterwards by emo black sheep daughter.

He had at least an hour before mum and older daughter would return and, he would hope, he had at least the same before the younger one decided to head back.

So, two additional cronies aside, the opportunity had presented itself. He would have to go with the armed robber who had a bit of a sadistic and psychotic streak. That was a fairly easy

95

role for him to play. There wouldn't be any need for method acting. *Draw on one's experience, darling.*

The greys of early evening were rapidly darkening, so Han quickly pulled on a balaclava and gloves. Courtesy of the Consortium, a morning courier had dropped off a separate package, which turned out to be a sawn off shotgun. It was the perfect accompaniment for his robber guise.

As he loaded both barrels, he headed down the side of the property, keeping an eye out for any nosey neighbours. He need not have bothered – the local residents were safely behind their castle walls and didn't seem to give a damn what happened beyond their own borders.

The rear of the property opened up into expansive and immaculately groomed gardens with lawns, mature borders and a covered swimming pool and hot tub.

Reaching the patio doors, he wondered absently whether the dossier may have left out anything important, like a guard dog. There was no evidence outside of one. He highly doubted that the Consortium would leave out a vital piece of information like that, but you never knew and Han wasn't the most trusting soul on the planet.

Visions of the Bryce family dog, hacked and decapitated sprung to mind, followed quickly by a fleeting image of Ju, his eyes downcast and forlorn, waiting for a master that would never return. He shook his head to dislodge the images.

He had no intention of killing another dog. Ever. Nor a cat, for that matter.

No cat or dog flap. A good sign, but certainly not concrete proof. The blinds were drawn on the patio doors and only revealed a few slivers of the kitchen beyond. After listening for a time, he tried the door and was not surprised to find it locked. He unlocked it with ease and then slipped inside.

The kitchen was set out in a large L-shape, with a breakfast area occupying the end section. The dossier had contained the plans to the house, so he continued across the room and paused at the door to the hallway. He could make out muffled chatter that sounded like it was coming from Greg's study.

He gently opened the door and moved along the hallway to the first door, which he knew to be the study. The talking grew louder.

"Tell the new kid he done good, Barry," Greg was saying. "Gave that black cunt what he had coming."

"Will do, boss."

"Give him this to keep him sweet. I think we should use him on another one."

"That's very generous of you, boss."

Han had to stifle a laugh. These fuckers had definitely watched far too many Guy Ritchie films.

He had heard enough. He stepped back and kicked the door with enough force to splinter the frame then stepped inside with the shotgun levelled on the nearest thug.

The two goons were stood in front of Greg's desk, with the man himself playing king on his tin pot throne.

"What the fuck—" was all that Greg could manage before Han pulled one of the triggers. The blast was deafening in the confines of the small office.

The big skinhead was thrown against the desk, knocking a banker desk lamp and digital photo frame flying. His leather jacket and shirt were shredded and thick gouts of blood spilled onto the Persian rug as he toppled over, clutching his bleeding abdomen.

The other thug had a fistful of bank notes, but he dropped them and went for something inside his jacket.

Han aimed the shotgun at him and said in his best comedy Cockney accent, "I wouldn't do that, my son."

The goon wasn't as stupid as he looked. He let his hand drop back down to his side and glanced over at his dying colleague on the floor who was choking on his own blood.

Greg had remained motionless, but now he found a voice. He looked down at the wad of bank notes on the floor that were fast becoming the epitome of blood money, then said, "Do you know who I am?"

Han kept the shotgun trained on the goon, but switched his attention to Greg. "Yes, as a matter of fact I do, Mr Rifkin."

"Well, you must be either thick as a fucking brick or have bigger balls than Barry here."

Han laughed, saying, "Oh, he would be called Barry, wouldn't he?" Ignoring their confused glances, he continued, "This is a simple business transaction, Mr Rifkin. I happen to know that you have around £100,000 in your safe behind that family portrait on your wall there."

Greg sat back in the chair with a look of bemusement. "You're gonna blag me, son? That what this is about?"

"That's right."

"You ain't getting a fucking brass farthing out of me, sunshine." He stood up and started moving around the desk. Han could see exactly what he was doing; widening the distance between his two targets, meaning that it would take longer to switch from one to the other. Han caught the merest flicker of an exchanged glance between the two men. He didn't wait for them to rush him. He pulled the trigger, blowing Barry back against a bookcase.

Greg ran at him. Han dropped the shotgun and slid the cosh down from his sleeve. It dropped neatly into his hand as Greg reached him. Han clipped him above the left eye, drawing blood and a yelp, Greg was a big man and kept coming, barrelling Han backwards against the doorframe.

The gangland boss managed to ram a hammer-like fist into Han's stomach, briefly arresting his attack. Wheezing, he managed to block the man's follow up blow and then brought his elbow down into the crease between shoulder blade and neck. As the man grunted, he jabbed at Greg's throat.

Coughing, the man flailed, which resulted in his fist connecting with the wooden doorframe. Skin tore away from his knuckle, exposing the bone beneath.

As he cried out in pain and frustration, Han kneed him in the groin and followed up with a head butt. Not exactly his finest fighting hour, but it had the desired effect.

Greg staggered backwards, cursing and spitting blood. Han moved in and battered him several times across the head with the cosh. His legs crumpled and he dropped to the floor, gasping and grunting.

Han rubbed his stomach and said, "You've still got quite a punch on you, slugger."

During the exchange, the first goon had let slip his mortal coil, but he noticed that Barry was trying to crawl towards the door, leaving a trail of blood in his wake. Han walked unhurriedly to him, saying, "And where do you think you're going, Barry?"

Barry turned his head to look up at the intruder. His face was contorted with pain, but he still managed a decent sneer.

"Say goodnight." Han stamped on his head repeatedly until he felt the skull give way under his boot. Fluid and brain matter spurted across the floor from his facial orifices. Barry stopped moving.

Turning back to Greg, he said, "Now that we've established who's calling the shots here, would you mind opening your safe now?"

Greg spat a wad of blood and mucus onto the floor and managed, "Fuck you."

"I could always ask your wife or daughters, if you'd prefer." He let the veiled threat hang in the air. He felt uncomfortable using it, but needs must. It had to look like a robbery in every detail.

Greg stared up at him through swelling bloodied eyes. "No! Alright!"

"Good lad."

Han dragged him over to the safe then helped him to his feet so that he could open it. He actually could have opened the safe himself, but appearance was everything, not to mention this way was a little quicker.

The safe revealed stacks of cash in £20 and £50 notes, along with a jewellery box. He quickly shovelled the cash into a bag then shoved the man back onto his chair.

"I'll let your wife keep her diamonds and pearls. She'll need them to console herself." Han laughed and added, "I can imagine she'll actually celebrate, escaping the pathetic clutches of such a clichéd second class thug like you."

"I'll find you and I'll—"

"Kill me?" Han finished, shaking his head in amusement. "So you've gone from Brick Top to Liam Neeson now then? I'd fucking pity you if I had an ounce of it in me."

Greg wiped blood and snot from his face and started to haul himself out of the chair, rage burning in his bloodshot eyes.

"You won't get the chance, old son." Han stepped closer and battered him over the head with the cosh a couple of times and then spied an ornate letter opener on the desk. He popped the cosh into his pocket and grabbed the six-inch silver implement.

"Mind if I use this?" he asked with an amiable smile.

"Fucking … cunt …" was all that Greg could manage between spitting blood onto his chest.

"You're a pal," Han said and then thrust it into Greg's eye.

The man twitched and thrashed as Han forced it right to the back of his skull then he abruptly fell limp.

As he took a moment to check that there was no pulse, he suddenly whirled around to see that the younger daughter was standing in the doorway, a frozen scream on her lips.

"Oh, bollocks," he said as she ran screaming from the room. It was a scream to rival Fay Wray's from King Kong. He grabbed the bag of money and headed straight for the front door. Time for a quick exit. As he opened the door, he shouted after the girl, "I'm sorry!"

Then he ran for it.

He drove to the waste ground that he had already picked out and torched the car, along with his balaclava and clothes. In fresh clothes, he then headed on foot to where he had stashed the second car. On the way, he dumped the shotgun and cosh separately in a stream and a hedgerow.

After that, he sauntered back to the apartment, stopping off to buy a coffee and muffin on the way.

Overall, he felt good about the outcome. It had been successful in every way, but it was a shame that the daughter had to witness her father being skewered like a kebab. That was most unfortunate. That would add a whole new level to her teenage angst. Maybe he should send her a copy of The Breakfast Club to help her with her counselling.

In the simplest terms, in the most convenient definitions. You see us as a brain, an athlete, a basket case, a princess and a criminal. Correct? That's the way we saw each other at seven this morning. We were brainwashed ...

Gabriel called as he walked into the apartment and congratulated him on a job well done. He agreed that it was unfortunate about the daughter, but it did lend credibility to the robbery story.

He also said that the money would be collected by a courier, as they could not risk him using it and the slim possibility of it being traced back to him.

"I'll put the Shelby GT500 order on hold then, shall I?" Han asked.

"Probably wise, but you could probably lease one."

"Not with the price of petrol these days," Han replied.

It was a shame, but Han wasn't exactly strapped for cash, so he just shrugged it off and spent a couple of hours shopping online for films and clothes instead.

***

The small cottage in the Cotswolds was set two miles outside the village, surrounded by rolling countryside that was shrouded in darkness. The cottage was a mere silhouette against the blackness, with only a solitary light in the living room as a single beacon amidst the sea of night.

Lionheart walked along the grass verge of the country lane, being careful not to step on the gravel.

This one seemed, on the face of it, a bit different. A white upper class Home Office civil servant. A hard-working family man doing his bit for his country. But that was all subterfuge. He was a traitor who had whored himself out to the Saracens. According to the powers that be, he was selling secrets to al-Qaeda. That made him far worse than the Saracen infidels – at least they were fighting a war they believed in, however unjust and blasphemous it may be. This traitor cared nothing for the war – he was selling out his brethren purely for financial gain.

So, not his usual Moor execution, but no less important to the cause. He had a good feeling about this assignment. On this one, he would be able to employ some of his creative juices that had been building up for far too long. He felt his pulse quicken in anticipation.

He picked his way towards the cottage, pausing every few yards to listen. The night was utterly still, expectant.

Lionheart carefully stepped in between some rose bushes and reached the living room window. Kneeling, he glanced through a narrow gap in the curtains.

The traitor liked to visit this place regularly for some solitude and to catch up on work away from the hustle and bustle of the city. Lionheart expected him to be sat at a desk, typing away. What he saw was not what he expected, but was by no means a surprise.

The traitor was pounding furiously into a petite young woman who was bent over a small dining table at the far end of the room. It must have been a spur of the moment act, as his trousers were around his ankles and her dress was thrown over her shoulders. They both were still wearing their shoes.

Lionheart shook his head sadly. The young woman did not look like the man's wife. She was at least twenty years younger and appeared to have full use of her legs, unlike the man's crippled wife.

The traitor had a Hugh Grant flop of hair and glasses that were giggling up and down with each thrust. His dossier had informed Lionheart that he was an obsessive runner and cyclist. His slim and toned body was a testament to that.

His eyes moved quickly from the man's thrusting buttocks and lingered on the woman's young firm form, following the slender curve of her toned, trembling legs. She too wore glasses and her brown hair was still in a tight ponytail. She was probably little miss sensible in the office. Not here though. He felt a hot stirring and his jaw clenched and unclenched in rhythm with the throbbing in his groin. She was colluding with the enemy. That made her a viable target. War was war.

He licked his lips and took a deep breath to calm his thumping heart then edged around the side of the cottage to the back door. His lock pick pouch was nestling in his coat pocket, but he didn't need them. He tested the door handle and it clicked open with a whispered groan.

As he slipped inside the kitchen, he heard the couple gasping their coital swan song.

"Oh, darling," the woman gasped, "I've missed you."

Moaning, then, the man, saying, "I've missed you too, sweetheart. Our times together are all that keep me going."

The door to the living room was ajar. Lionheart stood, staring through the gap, his eyes glowing from the reflection of the flames flickering in the open-hearth fire.

The woman was adjusting her dress as the man zipped up his trousers. They were giggling like schoolchildren. As they finished they flung their arms around each other and kissed passionately. Their faces were flushed and their eyes locked on one another, oblivious of the intruder watching them from a few feet away.

Lionheart stepped through the doorway and moved towards the couple at speed.

Whether it was the gentle creak of the door hinges or a groan of a floorboard, the man broke the embrace and glanced around. His frown turned to terror as his eyes widened upon seeing the intruder rushing towards them.

"What the—" was all he managed as the woman opened her mouth to cry out.

Lionheart backhanded the woman with enough force to lift her off her feet and send her tumbling over the leather Chesterfield, a jumble of flailing limbs.

To the man's credit, he leapt at Lionheart with fists raised. His actions were noble enough, but his eyes revealed crippling terror.

Lionheart didn't bother with his dagger. He had something altogether more unique for this man-whore. He jabbed the man in the throat and then slapped him with the blade of his hand under his nose.

The man staggered backwards, choking and his vision blurred. "Stop! Wait!" the man managed, clutching his throat with one hand and blindly holding the other out in front of him in a desperate attempt to ward off the intruder.

Lionheart swatted the feeble man's hand aside and drew close. As he gripped his head in a chokehold, he said, "Shhh ..." The man gurgled and then, in seconds, he went limp, unconscious.

Lionheart let the man drop to the floor and turned to the woman. She was whimpering softly and tentatively trying to drag herself onto her knees. Her glasses had been dislodged and her cheek and jaw were rapidly reddening.

"Good of you to prepare, my dear," Lionheart said, striding over to her and unzipping his trousers. "But do feel free to struggle. It's always more fun that way."

She was quickly gathering her senses after the blow and her groans turned to shrieks. "David! Oh, God!" She struggled to her feet and turned to run. Lionheart reached her first and punched her hard in the back of the head, dropping her in short order.

She was crying as he flung her light frame over the Chesterfield and yanked her dress over her head. He studied her quivering buttocks for a time, his tongue flicking in and out of his open mouth. "Your lover entered you gently in your filthy cunt. I will not sully myself with that, you whore." He pulled her cotton briefs aside and forced his way into her. As she shrieked, he added, "You will not enjoy this."

***

The civil servant moaned and began to stir. He quickly realised that his limbs were restricted and began thrashing his head back and forth, glaring feverishly around the room. Pain tore at his senses and then he heard screaming.

"David! Please!"

Without his glasses, he blinked and strained to make out the slightly blurred shapes in the room. The first thing that he noticed was that the Chesterfield was dangling above him by a thin, creaking rope. Then he realised that he was strapped over two dining chairs that were back to back. The solid oak backs of which were pressing into his lower spine. His arms were tied to the radiator near the kitchen door and his legs were tied to the front door, leaving him suspended and completely immobile over the chairs.

"David!" the woman screamed again.

The man craned his neck to see that his mistress was struggling to hold a rope that, via a pulley, was keeping the heavy sofa from dropping down onto him. She was bloodied and her dress was torn, revealing one small breast.

"Abbie! What did he do to you?" he cried, his voice straining over each word. "What the hell is going on?"

"I am delighted you asked," Lionheart said, stepping into view.

"Untie me, you bastard!"

"Why would I go and do that after taking so much time and effort to create this beautiful arrangement?" Lionheart asked, shaking his head in mock humour. "You have been lashed across two sturdy chairs with around one hundred and sixty pounds of Chesterfield suspended seven feet above you. Your whore is doing a sterling job of holding it in place, but I can see that she is starting to tire."

David turned back to the terrified woman. Her arms were shaking and her face was bright red. "Just lower it slowly, sweetheart. Don't worry, I'll be okay."

"Can't!" she cried, tears streaming down her face.

David's frantic eyes turned back to Lionheart. "What?"

"The whore is correct, I am afraid," Lionheart said, nodding sadly. "You probably cannot see from that angle, but there is a cook's blowtorch set a few inches above her hands and its trigger ignition is connected to the rope. If she lowers the settee more than an inch the blowtorch will ignite and incinerate the skin and flesh from her hands. I speculate that if the rope is not burned in the process, your dear little slut here will have no choice but to drop all one hundred and sixty pounds of Chesterfield onto your chest, thereby snapping your spine in two. *If* you survive, you will be crippled, just like your poor wretched wife."

"Is that what this is about? Betraying my wife?" David uttered weakly. "You don't understand! We haven't been able to have a physical relationship for years. She—"

"Spare me," Lionheart interrupted with a wave of his gloved hand. "This isn't about your wife. Your betrayal of her is disappointing, but would not warrant … this, if I may say, rather flamboyant display." He waved his hands around the room, revelling in his creation and laughing at the looks of horror the gesture garnered from his captive audience.

Craning his neck to draw the maniac's attention, David said, "What then? What do you want, damn you?"

Lionheart glanced over at the woman. She was fighting to hold the end of the rope just below the blowtorch. She was crying, but her teeth were clamped together in grim determination. "You're doing splendidly … Abbie, isn't it? Just … hang in there, if you'll pardon the pun." Turning back to David, he said, "This is about your betrayal of your country to the Saracens."

David appeared genuinely confused. "What? What the hell are you talking about?"

"Selling secrets to al-Qaeda. For that, you have been sentenced to death, which will involve a great deal of suffering in this life and the next."

"Selling secrets to *who*? What are you talking about? I work *for* the government! I am not a traitor!" His voice turning shrill, he added, "You've got the wrong man!"

"Your shameful and desperate pleas for clemency will not work on me – I serve a higher purpose. You have already been tried and found guilty. Make peace with God." Lionheart turned and left.

"I'm not a traitor, God damn it! This is all wrong! Wait! Come back!"

"David!" Abbie screeched. "I … can't hold it much longer!"

David opened his mouth to shout after the intruder one more time, but thought better of it. Instead, he twisted as much as his bonds would permit to take in every detail of the room and the rig the lunatic had created.

When nothing sprung to mind, he thrashed with every ounce of his strength. It was futile. The ropes just bit into his skin even tighter. Feverish and trembling, he turned back to Abbie.

Her wild eyes were staring up at the gently swaying sofa. She had managed to hook a foot around the radiator under the windowsill, which was helping a little, but she knew she could not hold it much longer. She choked back a sob as her eyes met David's.

"Fuck ... fuck ..." David uttered. "Can you ... erm ... what about tying it off on something? The radiator?"

"Already fucking tried that!" Abbie sobbed, snot mingling with her tears. "There's not enough rope!"

David struggled frantically again, but with the same result. "Fuck!"

"David ..." Abbie whimpered, her bloodshot eyes imploring. "I ... can't ... hold on ..."

David stared at her. Her slender arms were shuddering violently and her chest was heaving. It was plain to see that he was out of time. "Listen to me, sweetheart," he said in an attempt at a soothing tone. "It's alright. Just drop it. I'll brace myself for the impact. I'll be alright, I promise."

"No!" she cried. "I can't do that! I love you!" As she spoke, her hands started to inch upwards. "No! No!"

"Abbie! Let go! Please! Do it! NOW!"

"No!" Abbie's hands were dragged higher and the blowtorch suddenly ignited. The intense blue flame struck her right hand. In a second, skin and flesh shrank away, exposing bone.

The searing agony was too much. Her hands spasmed and the end of the rope shot up to the ceiling.

David was screaming Abbie's name as the Chesterfield plummeted down. One hundred and sixty pounds struck him midriff. His spine snapped like a twig.

In their desperation, neither had noticed the smell. As David became a paraplegic, the gas that Lionheart had left on earlier was ignited by the blowtorch.

A fireball ripped through the cottage and then, a moment later, the gas main exploded.

Lionheart was watching the cottage from back at his car when it blew apart, lighting up the dark undulating hills like a supernova. Dancing flames and burning debris shot high up into the night sky.

He watched for a time, fire burning in his eyes. Thoughts of battles long past filled his mind; battered castle walls, standards flapping in the wind, battle cries and thunderous siege engines. The whoosh of thousands of arrows streaking across the sky and the pounding of hooves from the approaching heavy cavalry. Smells of blood, sweat and shit filled his nostrils and he inhaled deeply.

A single tear trickled unnoticed into his beard and a smile touched his lips. "Beautiful," he breathed.

His satisfaction was short-lived. *The bedroom door clicked shut. Hot mint-scented breath on his cheek. Time for your lesson, boy …*

Lionheart closed his eyes and slowly drew in several deep breaths. He filled his mind with the image of the civil servant's mistress, of the Moor's wife, and a steady stream of nameless whores and victims. The bedroom faded as his arousal grew. He pictured their breasts smeared with blood and cum, legs thrust apart, holes violated.

He unzipped himself and pulled out his manhood. He rubbed hard and fast, grunting and hunched over, their naked abused bodies filling him completely. He ejaculated onto the dirt then zipped up.

He sneered at his semen then jumped into the car and drove off.

***

It took Lionheart two hours to drive to his isolated home on the edge of the Brecon Beacons in Wales.

His home comprised of a small converted village church. It had been a shell when he first discovered it, having been left to rack and ruin for a quarter of a century. He had spent two years rebuilding it, stone by stone, with his bare hands.

It did not have running water, electricity or gas, but that was just the way he wanted it.

The central nave had been partitioned and one section transformed into a kitchen and sitting area and the other into a workshop and storeroom. He had painstakingly restored the stone altar, which had pride of place at the head of the sitting area.

Lionheart deposited his rucksack on a workbench and then stripped naked. He picked up a cattail whip of knotted cords then walked across the stone flagstones to the altar. His back was crisscrossed with scars, marks and indentations, some old, some scabbed and still healing.

After crossing himself, he proceeded to lash the whip over his shoulder. Where it struck, angry welts immediately rose up, in places drawing beads of blood. He grimaced with each strike, but held his head up high and quietly praised the Lord.

After cleansing his body in the nearby brook, he dressed in a simple homemade robe and prepared supper. The storeroom had several pheasants and rabbits hanging up from his hunt the previous week. He plucked a rabbit down and effortlessly skinned and gutted it.

He fried the meat over his wood-burning stove with a selection of homegrown vegetables.

After eating by candlelight, he retired to the raised platform in the eaves that overlooked the sitting area. He sat cross-legged on his bedroll and read a few pages from a tatty and worn leather-bound King James Bible.

The pain had eased to a satisfying dull ache. He set the bible aside, placed his hands in his lap and closed his eyes.

He listened to the settling of the old building and the low moan of the wind blowing through the eaves. He emptied his mind and allowed sleep's tender embrace to take him.

LONDON

We are supposed to be righteous.

CHAPTER 8

The bar was packed with city suits well on their way to drowning their financial crisis sorrows on a Friday afternoon. Loud chatter, laughter and animated discussions filled the air.

Han made his way through the crowd carrying two pints. He handed a lager to Diego then took a gulp of his Guinness. There were no free tables, so they stood by a fruit machine.

"Cheers, mate," Diego said, taking a sip. "Another top session."

"Aye," Han said. "I'm really enjoying it."

Diego stared at him over the edge of his pint. After taking another drink, he said, "Even though I ain't got no one in your league?"

Han shrugged. "It's still good exercise and you know it's not about the competition aspect for me."

"Fair dos." Diego fell silent, lost in his own thoughts.

Han was distracted by a slender blonde in a short blood-red dress brushing by. An image of Cara on their first date, looking like Shosanna Dreyfus sprung immediately to mind. It felt like a stab to the heart. He looked away quickly and took another big gulp of stout.

"Nice," Diego said, with a nod towards the passing woman.

"Aye," Han muttered. Changing the subject, he added, "Best fight scene in a film?"

Diego sipped his drink as he considered the question. "Tough one that. It'd probably have to be the second last one in Enter the Dragon for me."

Han nodded approvingly. "Yeah, good choice. A bit predictable though."

Diego laughed. "Oh yeah? What would your choice be then?"

"It's a bit obscure, but do you know the John Carpenter film, They Live?"

"Nah, never heard of it."

"Philistine!" Smiling, Han continued, "There's a fight scene between Rowdy Roddy Piper and Keith David that is just epic. It must last over six minutes of the two of them pounding shit out of each other. For a fight fan, it's a must see."

"Sounds class, mate. I'll look it up." It was Diego's turn to change the subject. "Getting back to your fighting level, I've been thinking—"

"Dangerous," Han cut in.

"Cheeky twat," Diego said and laughed. "I know a couple of top class fighters who are always on the look out for a challenge."

Han took another drink then said, "I know where this is going."

"On their own they're good, but as a team, they're hard to beat. I think they might just be the kind of challenge you're looking for."

"Am I looking for a challenge?"

Diego stared at him. "Yes, I think you are."

Han mulled that over for a time, sipping his drink. Was he testing his training? Or was he just searching for the edge to see if he could throw himself off it?

Continuing, Diego said, "I could give em a bell – see if I could set something up. If you're game."

"To take on the two of them together?"

"Yeah. What do you reckon?"

Han finished his pint in silence. Then, with a shrug, he said, "Sure, why not." Handing his empty glass to Diego, he added, "And it's your shout."

***

As Han left the bar, a man wearing a crash helmet slipped a package into his hand and then disappeared into the crowd.

Han didn't bother trying to follow. He knew what it was immediately – he was starting to get used to the drill. A new assignment. He was quite surprised at being handed it outside a pub with dozens of people smoking and walking by though, but such was the dark and mysterious world he inhabited.

As if to answer his questions, his phone rang.

He answered it as he continued walking.

"Hi, Han," Gabriel said. "Sorry to catch you at such a late hour, but the assignment you've just been handed is a matter of urgency."

"No problem," Han said. "What's up?"

"We have identified a high level security threat for the Olympic games. We need to move fast otherwise we'll lose them and you're our only available asset at such short notice."

"Isn't the counter-terrorism unit or SAS supposed to deal with this sort of thing?"

"Unfortunately this lot slipped under their radar and to bring them up to speed will cost too much time. You are our only viable option."

"Okay then. Sounds like a ball."

***

Han grabbed a takeaway coffee and pastry on the walk back to his apartment, flicking through the dossier on the way.

This time, the dossier was somewhat lacking in detailed information, but the crux of it was that a terrorist cell linked to al-

112

Qaeda was planning to detonate several devices on the London transport network on the day of the games' opening ceremonies. The cell comprised of two North African males and a Middle Eastern female and they were holed up in rented flat in Brent Park, just off the North Circular.

It wasn't much to go on, but it was enough. To be honest, he preferred things when they were nice and simple anyway.

What it lacked in detail it made up for with the loaded Glock 17 pistol. It was an altogether more gentlemanly weapon than the sawn off shotgun for the Rifkin job.

Gabriel had told him to grab a couple of hours sleep and then head straight over there. There wasn't going to be any finesse or theatrics with this one. Just a bullet to each of their heads and then torch the premises.

Han decided that there was no time like the present. Instead of trying to sleep, he showered and downed another couple of cups of coffee to banish the residual effects of the five pints of Guinness. In less than twenty minutes, he was heading back out into the night munching on a slice of toast.

As he flagged a taxi down, his phone rang. Hopping into the back of the black cab, he told the driver, "Harlesden, please." He then took the call, saying, "Hi, Gabe, I know."

"We need you fit for purpose—"

"I'm fine. There's no way I would've been able to sleep anyway, so I might as well just crack on, eh?"

There was a pause then a sigh and Gabe said, "Alright. If you're sure. Good luck."

"Cheers."

It was still nearly a two mile walk from where the cab dropped him off, but it was safer that way. He walked at a steady pace, avoiding main roads and CCTV where possible.

It was still dark when he arrived, but there was only another hour or so until sunrise. It was a clear, chilly pre-dawn. There was silence, apart from the low grumble of distant traffic on the North Circular.

The flat was part of a converted semi-detached house on a well-kept street with neatly trimmed lawns. He had been expecting some sort of squat for some reason. He had had visions of having to pick his way through shit, piss and needles, so this was a pleasant surprise. Why he envisaged terrorists living like squatters was beyond him.

He was still shaking his head with mild amusement while he walked through to the rear garden. The back lawn was weed ridden and knee-high, with six-foot fence panels lining it on all sides. Nice and private.

There were two back doors. Terrorist Family Robinson were in the downstairs flat, so he checked for the correct door and quickly picked the lock. The door still didn't open. There must have been a deadbolt as well. Clever terrorists. It would have to be done the old fashioned way.

Han stepped back, raised a boot and kicked hard. The door and frame splintered. He shouldered it aside and stormed in, drawing the Glock as he stepped over the threshold.

He immediately heard shouts from further inside the flat as he moved through a clean and tidy galley kitchen. Neat terrorists.

A flabby bare-chested black male appeared in the hallway with a machete in his hand. His eyes widened at the sight of the pistol and he shouted something unintelligible to Han's ears.

Han opened fire, putting one round into his puffy face, splattering blood and brain matter across the hall and front door. He fired two more into his torso, the impacts causing undulating ripples in his fat. He dropped to the laminate floor, twitching, with blood quickly pooling around his corpse.

Han moved swiftly to the first door in the hall and kicked it in. An empty bathroom. As he turned to the next door, a second slim male and the Middle Eastern female both charged out of a bedroom to his side. The man was gripping the collar of a Rottweiler. As soon as the dog caught sight of Han it started barking and snarling.

As the man released the dog Han spun and fired off a snap shot, which blew out the glass in the front door, missing the wiry man by a couple of inches.

The dog leapt at him in the next instant, its owners not far behind. He managed to present his arm as the easiest target and the dog was good enough to oblige. Its jaws sunk into his arm and he clenched his jaw to stifle a cry.

He staggered back with it clamped onto his lower arm as it shook its head from side to side, tearing flesh. Without a choice, he punched it repeatedly in the side of the head with the butt of his pistol.

The dog yelped and released its grip, shaking its head.

The man and woman rushed past the dazed dog, flailing kicks and punches at him. Somewhere in the melee the pistol went flying.

Han backed up, blocking each attack, while his eyes searched for the Glock. Blood splattered the walls from his injured arm.

The woman bent down to pick something up as the man continued the assault. To Han's relief, she held the machete in her hands, rather than the pistol.

She screamed something possibly in Arabic and launched herself at him. She was slim and, under different circumstances, Han would have found her long raven hair and athletic frame quite appealing. As it was, her ordinarily attractive face was twisted with rage.

Han ducked and moved closer, the blade flashing overhead. It embedded into the wall and shattered a picture frame of a bland scenic view. He grabbed her wrist, twisted it and then brought his elbow down, snapping it like a twig.

As she shrieked in agony, the man landed several blows into Han's back and shoulders, forcing him to his knees. He whirled around in time to catch the man's foot as it was coming straight for his face. He twisted it, throwing the man off balance and crashing into the wall next to the machete.

The Rottweiler rejoined the fight, snapping at Han's leg. Teeth seized his boot and with one hard yank, it destabilised him and sent him flat on his face.

Even with her broken wrist, the woman came at him again, lashing out with legs and her uninjured arm. Han kicked out at the dog and swung onto his back to swat the woman's blows aside.

Another kick at the dog sent it reeling. He grabbed the chance to scramble back to his feet and promptly rammed the palm of his hand into the bridge of her nose.

There was a loud crack and she toppled over like a felled tree.

Han threw himself to one side as the machete cut through the air towards him. He hit the wall hard, but managed to turn in time to kick at the man as he moved in for another attack. He caught the man in the sternum, which sent him stumbling backwards.

He spied the pistol in the open doorway of the bedroom. He lunged for it as the man started at him once more.

He grasped the pistol as the dog's jaws snapped shut on the thin air where his missing fingers used to occupy. Ignoring it, he spun and fired. This time the round struck the man in the chest and punched him back against the wall. Jumping to his feet, he shot him twice more before turning to the prone woman. She was probably dead anyway, but he put a round into her now serene face, ruining those pretty features forever.

The dog came at him once more. Han aimed the pistol, but as it leapt at him, he changed his mind. Instead, he gripped the dog in a bear hug, avoiding its blood-stained teeth and applied pressure to its neck.

Its snarling and barking subsided. After checking its pulse, Han carried the unconscious dog out into the back garden, where he laid it down in the long grass at a safe distance from the house. "Rest easy, bud," he said to it before returning to the flat.

With no time to lose, Han rushed into the far bedroom and, popping a zippo, set fire to the curtains. They took hold quickly. He then rushed back into the kitchen and turned on all the gas rings on the cooker.

As he wrapped a tea towel around his bleeding arm, he turned to examine the rest of the kitchen for anything else to aid the process. The shrill tones of approaching sirens made the decision for him. He was out of time.

He ran into the back garden and sprinted at the rear fence, launching over it and into an adjoining garden. This one was in a far better condition than its neighbours, but Han didn't stop to smell the roses. He kept going at full sprint until he was far from the scene.

He didn't risk transport, instead he opted to walk all the way home, taking the scenic route through parks and using secondary roads.

It was at times like this that his thoughts would turn to Cara and their baby, but he was too drained even for that. Instead, his mind was filled with nothing more than the imminent prospect of feeling the loving embrace of his bed.

It was light by the time he trudged up to his apartment.

His phone rang as he stepped across the threshold. He accepted the call, but didn't have the energy to speak.

"Given the circumstances and timeframe, I'd say that was a job very well done," Gabriel said.

"Thanks."

"The gas explosion and fire didn't do as much damage as we would've liked, but that's only a minor detail."

Then why the fuck mention it then? Han thought, but managed to hold his tongue. Instead, he muttered, "Happy for ya."

"You must be exhausted," Gabriel said, stating the obvious. "I just wanted to thank you for completing a difficult job under tight conditions. You really stepped up to the mark with this one."

Han shuffled into the kitchen and poured himself a shot of whiskey. He downed it in one.

"I'll arrange a nurse for you first thing in the morning," Gabriel was saying. "Will you be alright until then?"

Han flung the sodden tea towel into the sink and rolled up his tattered sleeve to inspect the damage. Several deep lacerations were still bleeding. He sighed and said, "Yeah, sure."

After muttering a distracted goodbye, he cleaned and bandaged the wounds then promptly collapsed onto his bed. He fell sound asleep within seconds.

***

Gabriel put down his phone and rubbed at a sudden ache in his neck. Arching his back, he managed a weary smile.

He reached over to shut down his laptop, but stopped, his hand hovering over the touchpad. A new email had appeared in his inbox. He opened it and his eyes grew wide, staring at the screen with rising disquiet.

At once, niggling concerns had turned to cold hard certainty. He snapped shut the laptop, grabbed his coat and left the apartment.

As he headed for the basement car park, he pulled out his phone and dialled a number. The call connected instantly.

"I can meet for that coffee now," Gabriel said as he hurried down the concrete stairwell. After a curt okay, Gabriel hung up and dialled a second number. It went through to voicemail. "Damn it," he spat as he ended the call.

The car park was well lit, but deserted. He headed straight for his BMW, glancing around the whole time. As he closed the distance, he heard a door slam, the boom echoing off the bare concrete walls. He stopped and instinctively sidestepped over to a support column. Using the structure as partial cover, he scanned the basement for any signs of movement.

Rapid footsteps approached. Gabriel's hand slipped inside his jacket and clutched the handgrip of his pistol. He held his breath and waited, his jaw clenched and his muscles struggling against the imposed inactivity.

A man in a business suit hurried into view, his chubby face flushed as he puffed and panted. Gabriel kept his hand on his pistol, but pretended to be fumbling around his jacket for his mobile phone. The man rushed by, muttering under his breath, without so much as a curious glance.

Gabriel let out the breath he had been holding in then hurried to his car, his hand still firmly planted on his pistol.

***

It had been a particularly gruelling session at the club. Diego's two out of town fighters had turned up for their challenge. They were a couple of seasoned tournament fighters from Aberdeen and had probably grown up fighting sailors and oil workers.

When the two fighters were introduced to Han, the larger of the two, who had at least four inches on Han, immediately said,

"Diego, min, ah know you're sound, but ah dinna think this is such a good idea. This fucker looks like he's been raped by Edward Scissorhands. You sure you're not putting too much clart on this loon?"

Diego turned to Han. "You still up for this, mate?"

Han was weighing up the two men, taking in every little detail. One was leaner and fitter and the other bigger and stronger, but both were fluid and nimble. They also moved well together, like a unit, instinctively anticipating each other's actions. They were both covered in scars and tattoos and looked like they had served in the Royal Navy for a time as well. As he studied every muscle, he was already nodding. "Of course." To the two Aberdonians, he said, "I wouldn't waste your time. That would be extremely unprofessional."

The man shrugged. "If ye're sure."

As they limbered up, Han noticed the larger fighter's left shoulder dropped a little lower than the right, suggesting an old injury, but there was nothing to give away a possible weakness on the smaller one.

The Aberdonians didn't waste any time. They took the fight straight to him. Han moved to meet them to give himself more room to manoeuvre.

They circled then moved in, attacking from different directions. Han dodged a blow, parried another then dropped and rolled out of the way, coming up behind the larger fighter. He swiped his legs, but didn't manage to bring him down, so rolled and jumped up, striking at the man's weak shoulder. They exchanged blows then Han backed off as the younger one moved in to intercept.

Parrying blows from the younger fighter, he managed to dodge the larger until an opening revealed itself. He suddenly moved in, grabbed the man's arm and threw him hard to the ground onto his weak shoulder.

As the man yelped in pain, Han was already blocking and countering the smaller fighter. A blow to the side of the head forced the Aberdonian back with a ringing ear, just as his teammate rejoined the fray.

Han kept moving, blocking and parrying, wearing them down with a jab to the throat, a blow to the solar plexus, a kick to the back of the knee. The sparring continued for another three minutes when Han managed to drop the larger fighter onto his weak shoulder again and this time managed a knuckle jab into the hollow under his ear that rendered him out of the running.

As he sprung to his feet, the smaller fighter landed a kick to the side of his head. He dropped and rolled away, avoiding the follow up. His ear was ringing and a trickle of blood dribbled down his neck from the crease of his ear.

The minor success spurred him on, moving straight in for another attack. He came in with a combination of kicks and jabs, forcing Han back. He blocked and dodged until an opening presented itself where Han managed to squeeze another jab to the solar plexus in between the man's guard. That temporarily arrested his onslaught.

Han exchanged several more blows with him, before tripping and locking him into a strangle hold. After a few seconds of struggling, he tapped out.

The big Aberdonian was coming around as Han helped his partner to his feet.

Both men looked at him with a mixture of surprise and admiration. They both shook his hand and clapped him on the back.

"Braw, min!" they kept saying to him, Diego and each other.

Han was bruised and bleeding and knackered, but satisfied.

After cleaning up, they all headed down to the local pub for a few drinks. Most of the club members drifted off as the evening progressed, back to wives and girlfriends. The two Aberdonians were the last to depart, heading off to a strip club, leaving Diego and Han alone.

"Man, you would've been a legend on the circuit," Diego said, shaking his head as he cradled his beer.

Han smiled at him. "You're too kind, mate."

"If you're this good at your age, fuck knows what you would've been like in your prime."

Now Han laughed and said, "Thanks a bloody lot!"

Diego laughed as well, saying, "You know what I mean."

"You know, I appreciate everything you've done for me." *I don't mean the fighting,* Han mused, his thoughts turning to the old Tarantino wannabe as he sipped his pint.

"Now don't start getting soppy, you old tart!" Diego laughed. "I value talent and hope that I somehow help harness it, that's all."

"Well, you're a good bloke, Diego."

Diego rolled his eyes and said, "Oh yeah? Says the bloke who I just got two men to try to batter the crap out of."

Han laughed once more. "Well, yeah, aside from that."

***

As Han walked home through the dark, mostly deserted streets, he noticed that he had a missed call. It was an unrecognised number, so he assumed it to be Gabriel. He checked his watch. It was nearing midnight. Too late to return a call to a spy handler? He wouldn't have thought so.

Han dialled the number he had committed to memory for Gabriel. Before it started ringing, there was an almost inaudible click then a female voice answered after a single ring.

"Hello, Han, good to hear from you," the woman said cheerily. "Your call has been transferred as Gabriel is currently unavailable. How can I help?"

Han stopped dead and warning bells started clanging like Notre Dame in a hurricane. "Is Gabriel alright?"

"He's fine, just unavailable at this current time, thank you for your concern. So, how can I help?"

She was friendly and professional, but something just didn't seem quite right. "Oh, nothing major – just wanted to check to see if he knew when my next assignment might be coming through, that's all."

"I'm sorry, I don't have that information, I'm afraid. I will pass the request on and someone will be in contact tomorrow."

Someone? Not Gabriel?

"Is there anything else I can help you with, Han?"

He cringed at some stranger calling him Han. It felt and sounded very wrong. "No, that's okay, thanks for your help."

"My pleasure," the woman said then disconnected.

Han stood and stared at the phone for a time. Footsteps behind him drew him back to the present and he spun around, phone raised like a weapon.

A young woman let out an involuntary gasp of surprise and scurried by him, glancing nervously over her shoulder every few seconds until she was out of sight.

Han rolled his eyes and started walking once more, the questions running rampant through his mind causing his feet to drag their heels. Gabriel was off the grid. And *someone* would be in contact. What did that mean? Had something happened to him or was there some sort of bigger problem with the Consortium? Did this have anything to do with that rather curious past conversation with Gabriel? Or was he just being a little paranoid here?

That conversation played over in his mind. He had been probing, but also offering reassurance. He had been reflective, melancholy even, during their last couple of conversations. His usual high energy seemed to have escaped him. It seemed odd at the time – out of character – but now it felt like a piece of a jigsaw falling into place. Had he known something was up or something was coming then?

He had no other way of contacting Gabriel, so, unfortunately there was nothing more that he could do, other than wait and see.

As he approached his apartment building, a courier stepped out of the shadows with a package in hand. Han tensed, but approached with a smile on his lips. "Another late delivery?"

"We get these all hours of the day and night," the young courier said with a shrug.

Han took the package and went inside without another word.

As he poured himself a Jack Daniels, he pondered on the timing of the new assignment. His phone did not ring to explain another tense time-sensitive anti-terrorist job. So, this was just a normal assignment this time. Just being delivered a bit late ... He was starting to get a very bad feeling about all of this.

He knocked back a shot and ripped open the package. As he read through the documents, his eyes widened. He paused to pour himself another shot.

The new target was a gangland boss living in Torquay, suspected of drug and human trafficking. He was responsible for smuggling class A drugs and illegal immigrants in from North Africa. The law had been unable to make anything stick on more than half a dozen occasions, so it was time to take more drastic measures.

A couple more concerns were already starting to surface. One, the target was located in Devon, so it was taking him away from London, less than an hour after finding out that Gabriel was off the map, and two, the mobster ran a powerful, organised and particularly vicious crew that were well-trained and well-armed.

This seemed like a way of getting Han out of the way in more ways than just distance. Was this an effort to kill him off? If so, why? He had played the dutiful and successful little serial killer to the letter, apart from his minor indiscretions with Cara and Carol. Why would they dispose of him now? After so much effort had gone into bringing him back from the brink of death, training him and creating a whole new life for him. And, with the vast resources of the Consortium, surely there would be far easier ways to get rid of one pesky serial killer. They would have any number of capable 'assets' to do that sort of thing, instead of hoping that some smugglers would do their dirty work for them.

He had to be letting his imagination run away with him. Any number of things might be going on with Gabriel and the Consortium, but this scumbag was still a legitimate target. He was the infamous Han Whitman – he had taken down a whole prison ship, for Christ's sake.

He stood up and paced the room as he downed another shot of whiskey. He felt wired and agitated. There was no way that he would be able to sleep, not even with the magical powers of Jack Daniels. An old Frank Sinatra quote sprung to mind … *I'm for anything that gets you through the night - be it prayer, tranquilizers or a bottle of Jack Daniels.*

None of those were going to do it, not tonight. Frank had missed out one other option.

A quick search online brought up several local escort agencies. He perused some of the fine ladies and then called a mobile number.

He felt a twinge of guilt as a man answered. He had never gone to a prostitute before, but he *needed* some female company.

The polite man gave him an address only a couple of miles away and asked whether it would be cash or card.

Surprised, Han said, "Erm, I didn't know you'd take cards. Cash is fine, thanks."

The address led him to an unremarkable looking street of terraced houses. He found the right flat and knocked. As he waited, he felt a flutter of nerves and guilt. He was just about to turn on his heels when the door opened.

A young red headed woman in jeans and a t-shirt stood in front of him and offered him an easy smile. She was as dissimilar from Cara and Lisa as he could find. "Hi, I'm Danielle. The agency said you'd be coming over." Her accent had a hint of Welsh.

Han managed an awkward smile. "Hi ... err ... yeah. Sorry it's so late." *Sorry it's so late? What a prat.*

She laughed and it immediately put Han at ease. "Don't worry, my love. I don't keep normal office hours here." She stepped aside, saying, "Come on in."

Han stepped through into a comfortable lounge. Everywhere was pristinely clean and tidy, except for a couple of glamour magazines and DVDs lying around. He noted one in particular as a personal favourite.

Nodding to the DVD, he said, "I love Lost in Translation. One of Bill Murray's best in my opinion."

With a glint in her eye, Danielle said, "Yeah, Scarlett Johansson isn't so bad either." She put her hands on her hips and added, "But I don't think you came here to talk about movies."

Han half-laughed and shrugged. "No, I guess not."

"Let's get the awkward bit out of the way first. It's one hundred for half an hour. Will that be enough for you?"

Han raised his eyebrows. "Erm, yeah should be."

After taking the cash, she said, "Okay, where do you want me?"

Han laughed again and quickly said, "Sorry, I'm new to this sort of thing. But I suppose that's what they all say, eh?"

Danielle appeared to way him up for a moment and then said, "No, I can tell you're new to this. Don't stress, my love. Think of this as purely a business transaction and you'll be fine. I'm here out of choice. I'm not some addict trapped in the industry. I'm doing this to help put me through uni."

"Well … okay then," was all Han could think of saying.

She immediately pulled her t-shirt off to reveal small freckled breasts.

The embarrassment and guilt was replaced with a stirring that he hadn't felt for quite some time.

HAN WHITMAN

THE DEEP

DVD

Rum's not drinkin', it's surviving.

CHAPTER 9

The lovely Danielle played on his mind the next day as Han readied himself for the journey ahead. He had a renewed spring in his step and felt ready to take on the world, well at least a drug baron and his cronies.

He couldn't exactly call it making love, given the exchange of currency, but it had been a relaxed and unhurried act. In between, they had chatted over a cup of tea. They talked about her philosophy degree, films and the usual pointless, but enjoyable banter.

It had been just what Han had needed, and not just the sex. Just some pleasant female company. But the sex was good too, of course.

The Consortium had planned every detail of his trip to Torquay to exterminate Tyrone Cloche, including transport, accommodation and equipment.

He picked up a Ford Focus in an industrial estate on the outskirts of Reading – it wasn't a rental, so Han's guess was that it was an untraceable ringer. The boot was already fully loaded with everything that they had deemed he would need and, to their credit, Han was inclined to agree with them. Maybe this was a reestablishing trust exercise with Gabriel out of the picture? Maybe Gabriel had turned rogue and they had to get rid of him? It was a possibility, but Han was usually a good judge of character and Gabriel had come across as utterly sincere in his belief of the Consortium's ideals and goals. But then again, he was most likely an ex-spook and therefore an accomplished liar. One thing he was sure about was that there was nothing he was sure about anymore. Until he had more to go on, he would just have to continue playing along.

On the long drive along the M4 and M5, Han contemplated his target. Tyrone Cloche was a tall, broad-chested man of Jamaican descent. He came from a well-to-do family – his father had been an investment banker, mother, a university lecturer. He studied Economics and Philosophy at Oxford's prestigious Keble College. A keen sportsman, he excelled in rowing, cricket and rugby. Then, after university, he secured an enviable position in the City and was tipped for the top, but then everything changed.

He quit the job and set up his own business, importing and exporting goods from his motherland. This led to an arrest for trafficking class A drugs and a twelve month stretch at Her Majesty's pleasure.

He maintained his innocence throughout, but on his release, his business ventures took a different slant. He must have decided that he would rather be hung for a sheep, than a lamb and took up the trade for real. This soon progressed into human trafficking as well.

Although a suspect and the regular subject of investigation, he had never been successfully prosecuted since that first arrest. He now reportedly controlled approximately seventy percent of the drug trade into southern England and fifty percent of illegal immigration.

Quite a bounce-back from that first conviction, Han pondered.

With a long monotonous journey, it was unavoidable that his thoughts would eventually turn to Cara. He tried to fight it at first, returning to the easy embrace of the flame-haired Welsh beauty from last night, but it only postponed the inevitable.

Their baby would be due any time, if she hadn't already given birth. He could be a father by now. The thought both delighted and terrified him. Would the baby be a boy or a girl? Did he have a preference?

Of course, his thoughts or desires on the matter were all irrelevant. His child could and would never know him. Would Cara tell the baby anything about him? Probably not. She would probably make up some tale for the sake of the child. Would she romanticise it? Unlikely.

With that cold sentiment, Han cranked up the radio and concentrated on the road ahead, emptying his head of the tormenting voices. Marillion's haunting tune didn't help ...

Cause I know what I want, know what I feel, I know what I need, Daddy took a raincheck ...

Han stared at the radio, mouth agape. "Give me a fucking break," he snapped, switching stations with a sharp jab of a finger.

The temperature rose several degrees the further west he drove. The English Riviera was a popular tourist destination throughout the year and an unseasonably hot March was no exception. Temperatures had soared to the mid twenties as he drove along the coastal route into Torquay, with a clear sky above and a languid azure ocean sprawling to his left.

After passing Torquay Golf Club, he arrived at the cottage that was to be his base. It was a small two-bedroom holiday rental with a perfect view of the coast and, more importantly of Long Quarry Point, where Tyrone Cloche's fortress-like estate was set.

He stashed his gear in the cottage, taking care to stow the more sensitive equipment under the floor in the loft.

Han then changed into shorts, a Dr Gonzo t-shirt and hiking boots. He paused to stare at the mass of scar tissue on and around his knee. Even after all this time, it still sometimes caused him pause for thought. Will had made a first class job of it. It was beyond even the Consortium doctors to make it look vaguely normal again, but at least it functioned well. It still made him feel a little self-conscious and that irritated the hell out of him.

With a sigh, he placed small lengths of string in between the door and frame of both the front and back doors and then headed out with a Nikon digital SLR camera dangling around his neck.

The breeze coming in from the sea was enough to bring out Goose bumps on his arms as Han walked at a leisurely pace along the cliff top. He stopped frequently to inspect the views and terrain, taking plenty of photographs. The Consortium documents already contained a comprehensive photographic and blueprint file, but he wasn't about to rely on their intel alone. Not with Gabriel AWOL and who he was up against.

Cloche's estate was surrounded by ten-feet walls, topped with spiked iron railings. CCTV and motion sensors were the garnish. If Michael Biehn had been about, he was sure there would have been a few robot sentry guns dotted around as well – that's about all that was missing.

There would be guards and patrols with attack dogs within the grounds and the coastal side harboured vertical cliffs. It would be difficult, but not impossible to go over the wall, but there was a greater chance of detection. The less conspicuous choice was the cliffs. That meant a dingy to the small isolated stretch of beach below the cliffs and then a gruelling two hundred feet climb.

Thank God for all that extra fitness training and climbing he had been doing. He had the gear for a lead ascent, but that would leave him too restricted in case of complications, so he decided to opt for a 'careful' free climb. He could always use a cam or nut, if needs be.

He had seen enough.

***

After a few drinks in the local pub, the next morning Han hired a kayak, and, with a rucksack of climbing gear and supplies, headed off around the coast. He checked out the target cliff face first, photographing it extensively to work out the best routes later. As was the law of Sod, it was the tallest cliff face for miles, so Han made do with a hundred feet face a couple of miles down the coast for his trial runs.

He dragged the kayak up onto the narrow stretch of beach then spent a couple of hours climbing up and down. Apart from one close call where he nearly lost his grip, he managed competently enough.

He was drenched in sweat as he sat on a rock on the beach and ate a sandwich. He stared out beyond the lapping surf to the vast stretch of blue. The English Channel was desolate, apart from a single ferry on the horizon.

His thoughts, once again, returned to Cara. No amount of imagining Danielle's soft, pale skin beneath his touch could shift it.

To the distant ferry, he said, "I just can't get you out of my mind." With a snort, he added, "Great, now I'm quoting Kylie, of all people. What the fuck is happening to me?"

With a sigh, he tossed the half-eaten sandwich into the surf and watched as a couple of gulls swooped down to claim it.

***

That night, Han headed out in a second hand kayak he had found advertised in the Herald Express. The darkness was silent, except for the rhythmic sounds of the sea.

Despite the cool sea breeze, he had managed to work up a sweat by the time he had paddled to the small stretch of beach at the foot of Cloche's cliff.

Pebbles crunched under foot as Han dragged the kayak up out of the surf. As the sea lapped at his ankles, he pulled out a pair of image intensifying binoculars and scanned the cliff top. He half expected to see a German soldier smoking a cigarette, while keeping an eye out for the Allied invasion. The thought brought a smile to his face – the first genuinely spontaneous smile for some time. His white teeth contrasted against his blacked-out face.

Tonight, Matthew, I'll be Gregory Peck, he mused to himself. Still smiling, he adjusted his black bob hat and moved over to the rock face. Just above eye level, there was a wide ledge before the main face rose up above him, so he hoisted himself up onto that for his starting point.

After checking that his gear was all secured, he took several deep breaths as he chalked his hands and then started his ascent.

He climbed with unhurried grace up the pre-planned route he had decided upon from the earlier surveillance photographs, only deviating by a handhold or two, here and there.

As he climbed, he was conscious that it would be a somewhat inglorious end to his otherwise illustrious career to end up slipping and breaking his neck on a solitary rock face in Devon. He would never live it down. He took his time, not leaving anything to chance.

He had picked out two break points to rest up, before continuing the ascent. The final break point was only four moves from the top, chosen on purpose to allow his body to recover before the real fun began. It also gave him a chance to listen for any activity.

As he reached the final break point ledge, the wind began to pick up, drowning out any possibility of hearing anything from above. It was irritating, but not unexpected.

As he rested, he ate an energy bar and drank a bottle of water. Glancing out to sea, he noticed a cloudbank on the horizon. He didn't fancy climbing back down the cliff in a storm. *A gathering storm*, he thought absently. *I am ready to meet my Maker. Whether my Maker is prepared for the ordeal of meeting me is another matter.*

There was the briefest flicker of lightning in its midst, like a single heartbeat. It was both a beautiful and ominous sight. Portents didn't usually hold much sway with him, but it was difficult to dismiss.

He forced himself to look away from it to continue with the job at hand. He finished his snack and stashed the rubbish into a deep crevice to avoid leaving what Andy McNab would call 'sign'.

After a few more breaths, he reached up to the next handhold.

He hauled himself over the final lip and lay flat in the grass, panting. The house and the perimeter were well lit, so he kept himself pressed against the cold ground as he surveyed his surroundings.

It didn't take long to catch sight of a sentry standing by an entrance to the rear of the expansive property, sipping a steaming drink from a thermos mug. Other than the loan guard, the grounds appeared to be deserted.

He had memorised the positions of the cameras and sensors, so he set off low at a sprint towards the house. As he zigzagged along a predefined blind spot path, he kept his eyes on the sentry.

The sentry was looking out into darkness, but Han wasn't about to take any chances. As he glanced his way, Han dropped flat to the ground and remained perfectly still. He continued to stare for a time then took another sip of his coffee. Grimacing, he cast the lukewarm dregs onto the lawn. He turned away, searching for his flask.

Han jumped up and continued. He reached the side of the house and crouched down amidst the shrubbery just out of sight. As he un-slung the MP5 submachine gun from his back, he kept glancing behind him, checking the side of the house for the perimeter patrol that he knew was out there somewhere.

He had practiced with a few different submachine guns during training, but this would be his first time using one in the field. *In the field?* he thought to himself. He was starting to sound like some sort of bloody secret agent! He rolled his eyes and flicked the safety to semi-automatic. *This was going to be fun!*

Han leaned around the corner, gun first, aiming down the scope. The sentry had poured himself a top up and was staring out to sea towards the storm, his expression reflective. He wasn't your Hollywood movie-type goon. He had a slender frame, glasses and a calm, intelligent face.

Looks could be deceiving, Han mused as he sighted the man's temple and squeezed off a single shot. The 9mm round struck the side of the man's head, jerking it to the side with the impact. He dropped to the ground. The suppressed report and the thump were all but drowned out by the wind and the surf.

Han moved quickly to the body and dragged it into a nearby copse of swaying palm trees. He tossed the flask in after him then glanced down at the spattered stain on the terracotta stone. There was no time to mop it up. It was enough to fool a cursory glance, which would be all he would need for now.

He paused at the door, straining to listen. What aided his first kill now hindered him. He could not hear a damn thing. There could have been a platoon of ice giants partying with the Incredible Hulk on an acid trip and he would've been non the wiser. *Fuck it.*

Still semi-crouched, he opened the door and slipped inside, tracking left and right.

***

A black BMW lay dark and motionless in a lay-by five hundred yards away from Long Quarry Point. Behind the blacked out windows two suited men sat in silence.

The passenger was scrutinising the display of the GPS tracking unit in his lap. "Target has breeched," he said with a brief glance to his colleague.

The driver offered a curt nod, but remained quiet.

A figure appeared in front of them, ghost-like against the dark backdrop of the coastline. The person dropped a long cylindrical device into the waiting tripod that had been carefully placed earlier just below the driver's eye line.

As the driver opened his mouth to shout a warning, the figure opened fire. Heavy machine gun fire peppered the windscreen. The bullet resistant glass was designed to withstand up to 5.56mm NATO rounds. These rounds disintegrated it as if it were ply board.

The passenger rocked in his seat as round after round ripped into his chest. Blood and glass splattered in all directions.

The driver managed to draw his pistol just as rounds danced in his direction. One struck his jaw and took his head clean off. It flew into the back amidst a spray of crimson.

The figure dismantled the M2 machine gun and left without a word.

***

The door led into a dark utility and storage room with workbenches, chest freezer, fridge and a washing machine. With no

133

immediate threat, Han stood and closed the door from the elements. Silence caressed him.

He moved quietly to the door ahead. A sliver of light pierced the crack below it.

At first, he heard nothing. Then a cough, followed by a clattering of pans.

Han pushed the door open and moved quickly inside. The kitchen was big enough to serve The Ivy. A stocky cook was clearing away pots and pans with his back to Han. He glanced over his shoulder, saying, "You can't be finished–" His sentence was cut short as he caught sight of Han and the gun trained on him.

Han opened his mouth to speak, but the cook moved quickly, ducking behind an island workstation and going for a sidearm. Han opened fire, squeezing off three rounds. Two splintered the granite worktop, but the third clipped the cook's forehead, flipping a large hunk of scalp and black hair up over the back of his head. He dropped to the ground, blood quickly pooling around his twitching body.

The reports were unmistakeable in the confined space, despite the suppressor. He had to move fast.

He jogged across the room, pausing only to put another round in the twitching cook. As he neared the far door, he heard shouting and running footsteps. He dropped into a crouch, tucked the stock tight into his shoulder in preparation and switched to fully automatic.

The door burst open and two suited figures rushed in, pistols already drawn.

Han squeezed the trigger. The remaining twenty-six rounds were spat out in two seconds flat. Both men were shredded in the volley, blood and chunks of flesh flayed from their bodies. Most of the door and doorframe disappeared with them.

Han released the spent magazine and reloaded as he moved past the splattered gore that was the remains of the two guards.

The doorway led into a hallway with a grand sweeping staircase that was now adorned with a fine mist of crimson and scattered bullet holes. He was loving this MP5!

A suited oriental woman had stopped midway down the stairs and was aiming a pistol right at him. She opened fire as he rolled to one side. Bullets tore up the tiled floor around him. Back on his feet, he returned fire, splintering the ornate banister. She jumped down the remaining stairs, firing until her pistol clicked empty.

As she frantically reloaded, Han put a three round burst into her chest. She slammed against the wall then slid down into an ungraceful squat, a smear of blood oozing down the wall after her. As red flowers bloomed on her chest, she twitched once then lay still.

"Kim!" a voice yelled from the first floor.

Han glanced up to see Tyrone Cloche glaring down at him. The big man was wearing a white unbuttoned silk shirt and linen trousers. He was as bald as Telly Savalas.

"I'll kill you, you motherfucker!" Tyrone spat, aiming what looked like a gold-plated Desert Eagle.

Han threw himself through a doorway as the drug lord opened fire. Bullets struck the frame and ricocheted off the tiled floor. He jumped to his feet to find himself in the dining room, its centrepiece a mahogany dining table large enough to sit two football teams.

He could hear Cloche thundering down the stairs, roaring an illegible battle cry.

Han quickly reloaded and moved around the side of the table, aiming at the door.

He heard Cloche thump against the wall, but he did not appear in the doorway. Instead, with his voice rasping from the scream, he said rather more evenly, "Before I be killing you, tell me who sent you?"

"You're pretty sure of yourself," Han said with a snort, maintaining his aim on the door.

"If you tell me, I will make it quick, bwoy," Cloche continued.

"Not much of an incentive."

"If you be thinking that you will kill me then what does it matter if you tell me or not? Either you die and it doesn't matter or I die and it still doesn't matter either."

Han shrugged. What did it matter? "You won't have heard of them, but you've pissed off some people in very high places."

135

Han heard the man suck in a breath. A fist slammed against the wall. "Tell me, God damn it!"

"The Troy Consortium."

"I prayed that it could not possibly be true," Cloche muttered.

"Oh, so you have heard of them." Han frowned. For a clandestine outfit, they were getting rather popular. Something suddenly felt wrong.

"Of course I have heard of them. I work for them."

Han unconsciously lowered his submachine gun. *What the fuck?* "That's bullshit."

Cloche stepped slowly into view, his pistol hanging limply to his side.

Han aimed at his head, but his index finger remained hovering over the trigger.

"I was beginning to get suspicious when ..." Cloche stopped and his eyes widened. "Take cover!"

Han was about to say that there was no way that he was going to fall for something as lame as that when the two stained glass windows exploded inwards, showering him with colourful shards. He dropped and rolled under the table as machine gun fire tore into the room, riddling the table and shattering chairs.

Cloche had also thrown himself to the ground and joined him under the table. "These be friends of yours?" he yelled over the gunfire.

"Cops?"

Cloche laughed. "With machine guns?"

"And I suppose they're not your reinforcements then?" Han said, growing more concerned by the second.

"Need I be reminding you that they're shooting at me also, breda?"

"Just spit-balling here!"

A small metallic object clattered to the floor a few feet away.

"Leg it!" Han yelled as he scrambled for the door.

The blast propelled both men through the opening and sent them reeling into the hallway.

Han pushed himself to his feet and winced at a sharp pain in his thigh. Glancing down, he saw blood seeping through a tear in his trousers. "Fuckers!"

Cloche glanced at Kim, dead against the wall then grabbed Han by the shoulder. "You'll live. We have to move." With a nod towards Kim, he added with a snarl, "We'll be finishing this later."

Cloche was half-dragging Han towards the kitchen when the front doors burst inwards with a splintering of wood. One door skittered across the hall and the other hung loose from one hinge. Two figures rushed inside, shrouded in swirling smoke.

Han stumbled towards the kitchen, skidding on the smeared gore in the doorway, as Cloche turned to cover their retreat. The Desert Eagle boomed behind him as Han entered the kitchen, startling a figure who was checking the body of the cook.

The man was dressed in full black tactical dress, complete with helmet, webbing and an MP5. He looked like American SWAT, except he was missing any form of insignia.

Han emptied a full magazine into him, catapulting him into a kitchen unit with such force that he split the door in two. His body armour had saved his life, but he was badly winded and bleeding from bullet wounds in an arm and a leg. Despite his injuries, he managed to bring his submachine gun to bear as Han struggled to reload.

Cloche entered and shoved Han to one side. He opened fire and the single shot split the man's goggles in two and sprayed blood and skull fragments across the kitchen units.

Cloche let the spent magazine clatter to the floor and reloaded as he manhandled Han through to the utility room. Behind them, gunfire erupted through the doorway from the hall as Cloche slammed the door behind them.

"I'll be hoping you had an adequate exit strategy," Cloche said.

Han glared at him. "No, I thought I'd go out guns blazing, like Butch Cassidy and Sundance, you prick."

"You can be quite the sensitive one. It is I that should be the irritated one here, breda, fucking with ma soap catch-up night."

"You're not exactly Scarface, are ya?"

"A little quips saltwater nigger? No, bwoy."

Shaking his head, Han went for the door handle. Cloche grabbed his hand as he started turning it. "This be a Consortium hit squad we are dealing with here. They'll be having snipers out there covering all the exits while the assault team clears the house."

More gunfire in the kitchen, followed by a shuddering blast.

"Well, we can't stay here. What do you suggest?"

The two men stared at each other for a moment, Cloche aiming at the door to the kitchen. With a sigh, he said, "We have no choice."

"I'm glad we agree on something," Han said and swung the door open. "Head for the cliff – I've got a kayak."

"You scaled your monkey ass up *that* cliff? You're head nuh good, breda!"

"I work for the Consortium. What the fuck do you think?"

"You got a good point there."

The two men ran out into the night. The wind had picked up since his time inside the house and rain was lashing down from the heavens. They headed for the cliff, Cloche quickly moving into the lead due to Han's injured leg.

Two men emerged from the rear entrance and opened fire. Bullets tore up the lawn around Han as he ran. He caught sight of several muzzle flares up ahead and the firing from the house ceased. As he grew closer to the cliff, a figure materialised out of the undergrowth. Initially startled, Cloche aimed at the man, but then lowered his pistol.

Han caught up with him and strained to make out the person. He was dressed in a black jumper and trousers and was cradling a sniper rifle. He pulled off his balaclava and smiled.

"Gabriel?" Han exclaimed, dumbstruck. "What the fuck is going on?"

"Damn good to see you, breda," Cloche said, taking the man's hand in his.

"Good to see both of you," Gabriel said, the wind whipping his hair into his face as he shook Cloche's hand vigorously. He then turned to Han. "All in good time, Han. I took out your tail earlier, but you're both bugged up to the nines. Dump *everything* and strip naked."

"I usually ask for at least a drink first," Han said.

"We haven't got time for jokes." Gabriel bent down and pulled out two tracksuits from a duffel bag at his feet. "Put these on."

Both men quickly stripped while Gabriel covered them.

A figure came into view, tracking around the perimeter of the house. Kneeling, Gabriel aimed and squeezed off a single round. The man's head disintegrated and the body dropped to the ground.

As they dressed in the tracksuits, Gabriel said, "I've got a car waiting. I've already taken the liberty of disposing of your kayak. Your cottage is compromised too, so we have to move quickly."

***

As they headed north on the M5, Gabriel filled them in.

"I have been getting concerned about some of the recent contracts over the last few months. The final proof came when I heard about the murder of a particular Home Office civil servant whom I knew to be one of ours."

Han finished tying off the field dressing to his leg and turned to Gabriel. His handler did not take his eyes off the dark road stretching out ahead of them. "What the hell does that mean?" Han asked, but he already had an idea what the answer would be.

"It means, Han, that the Consortium has become corrupted. How or why doesn't matter at this point. I knew I would be a target, so I promptly disappeared. I also knew that as soon as I fell off the grid the Consortium would initiate the Clean Sweep Protocol."

"I can fucking guess," Han muttered.

"He be catching on quick, your bwoy here, you say?" Cloche said from the rear seat, glaring at the back of Han's head.

"So they started taking out all of my assets," Gabriel continued. "Particularly sneaky of them to get you to try to kill Tyrone, Han. Tyrone has been one of my most trusted assets – and a good friend – for several years."

"So the bastards get me to do their dirty work, eh? One of us kills the other and then their team moves in to take out the survivor. It's a win-win for them. Motherfuckers!"

"Your bwoy here murdered Kim," Cloche said, the whites of his eyes glowing in the darkness, as if boring right through Han's head.

Han turned around to face him. He pulled his hat off and absently scratched his scalp then said, "My bad."

"I'm sorry, Tyrone, I know you two were close," Gabriel interjected. Glancing at Han, Gabriel said, "It wasn't Han's fault. They used him."

"Someone *will* pay," Cloche muttered, continuing to stare at Han.

"So now what?" Han asked, dropping back into his seat.

"Well, all good parties come to an end, but as luck would have it, I had planned for this eventuality." As an afterthought, he added, "I never thought it could ever happen …"

"Nice of you to invite me along," Han said.

Gabriel ignored the quip. "Together with a select few like-minded people, we made a pact that if or when the Consortium failed to live up to its ideals then we would make it our mission to take it apart."

Han stared at him, incredulous. "You've got to be fucking kidding me."

Gabriel stole a moment to look Han straight in the eyes. "No, I'm deadly serious." Turning back to the road, he added, "The Consortium is capable of great good, but rotten and unchecked, it is capable of absolutely anything. It's my worst bloody nightmare."

"Trapped at a Bieber concert would be mine," Han said.

Gabriel managed a thin smile, but it evaporated immediately. Watching him, Han couldn't help but notice the physical changes the man had gone through since their last meeting at his apartment. Deep furrowed lines were etched into his normally cheerful face and his eyes were sunken and bloodshot. He clearly hadn't slept or eaten properly since the civil servant's murder.

"I be thinking that most people would go for clowns?" Cloche injected. "Or a zombie apocalypse?"

Han glanced over his shoulder. "A zombie apocalypse? Are you kidding? That would be the best thing that could happen to this fucking planet. I'd be in my fucking element. Bring it on, I say."

Cloche stared at him with a mixture of disquiet and amusement. "I have no idea why the Consortium would recruit you – you be having such a healthy respect for life and all."

"Says the drug dealer."

Cloche leaned forward. "You do not have any idea what you are talking about, white bwoy."

"Okay, guys, can we get on the same team here?" Gabriel said.

Han turned back to Gabriel. "Okay, so I can understand that you want to try to take them down, but I'm new to all this. None of this shit really has anything to do with me."

Gabriel took his eyes off the road for a moment to stare at him. "Do you think?"

"I could just get the hell out of Dodge – disappear for a few decades."

Gabriel shook his head, his eyes back on the road. "There is nowhere you could hide, no distance that you could travel and no length of time that could pass that would stop them from tracking you down and eliminating you." With a sigh, he added, "This now has everything to do with you, whether you like it or not."

Han stared at the dark road stretching out ahead of them as he contemplated the true gravity of the situation.

Gabriel broke the apprehensive silence. "The Consortium is going to send *everything* after us. It's open season. Whether we like it or not, all we've got here is each other."

"So much for my lone gunman persona," Han muttered. Trying to lighten the mood, he added, "My psych evaluation read, 'does not work well with others'. Just thought I'd mention."

"Mine read, 'aggressively protective of loved ones and single-minded in the pursuit of righteous retribution against any fool who would be fucking stupid enough to harm them'," Cloche said without humour.

"I can see this is going to be a fun trip," Han replied with a sigh, but he was at least a little happier at having managed to get under the man's skin.

Han sat back and closed his eyes, listening to the drone of the engine. His thoughts were filled with the events of his life and his journey so far. He thought about all of the people who had shared that journey, some fleetingly, most no longer living. Images of his mum, brother ... even his dad ... played in his mind. Those pictures were joined by Perry, Lisa, John, Carol, Jimmy, Sam, Big Joe and Mandy. Still more followed; Diego, Amwolf, Danielle and finally ... Cara.

He imagined her sitting in the bay window in her flat, where the sun used to cascade through in the morning. She was sat, a look of dreamy contemplation on her face, one hand holding a cup of coffee and the other caressing her swollen belly.

Jumanji's nose appeared, nudging his new master's leg for attention. She looked down at him and smiled as the dog's head rested in her lap. She set her cup down and gently rubbed behind his ear.

***

Near Chippenham, Gabriel pulled onto a narrow country lane, which led to what, at first glance, appeared to be a disused farm. As they pulled up to a barn, a figure stepped out of the shadows to open the doors. Han didn't recognise him, but he offered a nod of recognition to Gabriel.

Gabriel drove into the barn and the man closed the doors behind them.

They filed into the farmhouse. Like the rest of the small holding, it seemed to have been derelict for some time; creaking floorboards, peeling paintwork and a scattering of dusty old furniture. A breeze was blowing in through the broken windows. Contrary to its appearance, several people were waiting for them in the flickering candlelight. The mood was subdued and apprehensive.

A man appeared from the kitchen, where there was a working wood-burning stove. Finally, someone Han did recognise. "Would you like a cup of tea?" Amwolf asked them with a welcoming smile.

"Love one," Han said. "They roped you in too, eh?"

"No roping was necessary, I assure you."

"Sounds like you're missing out there."

Amwolf laughed. "You creak me up."

"I think that's crack, mate," Han said with a chuckle.

Gabriel glanced around the room, his expression pinched. Turning to a tall, almost Amazonian woman, he said, "Good to see you, Maggie. Is this it?"

There was relief in her smile. "Afraid so, Gabe. We've got a couple of MIAs, but Jonah, Pepe, Clarence and Shelly are all gone."

Gabriel slumped down into an armchair, disturbing a cloud of dust. "Christ," he muttered under his breath.

"The Clean Sweep Protocol must've been more far-reaching than even we imagined," Maggie continued. "Anyone – and I mean *anyone* – who the Board deemed questionable in the slightest has been eliminated. It's been a fucking slaughter out there. I barely got out myself."

Han noticed a graze on her cheek and a limp as she crossed the room to give Gabriel a hug. He rose and held her in his arms for a time. As she moved away, Han caught her swiping a tear away from her eye.

"What are we going to do, Gabe?" a man by the window asked, fidgeting from one foot to the other. He constantly switched his attention from Gabriel to the grimy window with half a pane of glass missing.

"We made a pact," Gabriel said evenly. "We take the Troy Consortium down or we bloody well die trying."

"How the fuck can we possibly do that now?" the man continued, stepping closer. His eyes were wide with fear.

Han leaned against the doorframe and observed the exchange with interest. Amwolf handed him a mug of tea then walked into the room to stand side by side with Gabriel. "We all made the pact, Robert. We are bound by it, so we have no choice but to try."

Robert ran a trembling hand across his brow. "They got Andrea and the kids ..."

Gabriel stepped towards him, but Robert raised his hand and retreated back to the window. "I'm so sorry, Robert." After a deep breath, he turned back to the group. "There's not as many of us as we would have hoped, but we can still do this. We've got Tyrone and Han to help us as well and they're two of the best."

"How can we trust *him?*" a lean, silver-haired man in cargo pants and a t-shirt asked with a nod towards Han.

"Thanks for the vote of confidence," Han said with a smile. Glancing to Cloche, he added, "Well, at least you're okay."

Cloche remained silent as the man added, "No offence, but I know your function, pal."

"I can vouch for Han one hundred percent, Zach," Gabriel said.

"It's alright, Gabe," Han said. "I don't need you to defend me." Han set his mug aside then straightened up and folded his arms, staring at the Colonel Quaritch replica. "Look, mate, I've been royally fucked and dropped in the meat-grinder just like the rest of you. I'm not looking for any cosy friendships and snuggling on the sofa with a nice Robert Pattinson movie here, but I am looking for a big fucking dose of payback. It's the only way I'll be able to have any kind of life after this great big fucking mess."

He locked eyes with the older man and, after a moment, added, "Is that okay with you?" He picked up his mug and took a sip of tea, not breaking eye contact for a second.

Zach folded his arms and offered a noncommittal shrug.

"What's the plan, Gabe?" Maggie asked, making her feelings clear to everyone.

"After Clean Sweep, the Board will meet as a matter of urgency to discuss the situation and their strategy moving forward. I am waiting to hear from a source on the date and venue of that meeting."

"They'll have tighter security than the fucking Olympics," Zach said.

"That's not hard," Han added.

144

"Han, please," Gabriel said, with a disapproving glance. Turning back to the rest of the room, he continued. "It will be our best and probably our only chance of eliminating the entire Board in one go. Otherwise, it could take us years to track them down individually."

"Will your source be reliable?" Zach asked. "And more importantly, can we trust him *or* her?"

Gabriel studied Zach for a moment. Han caught a flash of uncertainty in his eyes, but it was gone in an instant. "The source is one hundred percent reliable and trustworthy. For security, you can understand why I can't divulge any other details."

Han's scrutiny turned to Zach. The man nodded, but his jaw clenched, in what could have been annoyance or frustration. He glanced around the room. These were the rogues and the outcasts, but Gabriel had already implied that they still had at least one spy within the Consortium's ranks, so what was the likelihood that they also had a traitor within the rogue camp? Likely. Probable. Fuck. He had seen Gabriel consider the same thing as he studied Zach.

So, where did that leave Han? The same as always – not trusting a God damn soul.

Interesting times, as the Chinese would say.

As discussions continued, Han stepped outside and found Amwolf staring up at the night sky, watching clouds roll by overhead. The man was clearly cold in just a sweatshirt, but he didn't show it. He just stood there, still, arms folded.

"Fun and games, eh?" Han said, joining him. "Looks like the storm's heading this way."

"A clear sign of our road ahead," Amwolf muttered, without taking his eyes off the sky.

"How deeply profound of you," Han said and winked at his former tutor as he fired him an irritated sideways glance.

Amwolf managed a half-laugh. Continuing to stare at the sky, he said, "I have not touched a cigarette in twenty-five years, but I could use one right now."

"Sorry, can't help you there, mate," Han said, shoving his hands into his pockets. "I used to smoke socially many moons ago, which is code for never wanting to buy my own."

Amwolf finally turned his attention to Han. Fixing him with a probing stare, he said, "Why are you here?"

"Gabriel's timing was impeccable," Han said. "And he gave me a lift."

Amwolf sighed. Han watched his breath plume in the cold air. "Why are you *still* here?"

Han mulled over the simple question for a time. "I'm not quite sure, to be honest. It's partly because I know I'm now a target anyway – and I dislike being anyone's target." Han thoughtfully scratched the stubble on his chin before continuing, "You know, it's also just a little bit bloody irritating. I was just getting used to the new life – it took some time to adjust, but I had just about accepted it and now all this bollocks happens. I mean, for fuck's sake!"

Amwolf shook his head sadly. "So this is all an inconvenience for you?"

Han shrugged. "Yes, it is, but it's not just that. It's like the time I met my last girlfriend – you know the one I told you about, the one outside the bar?"

Amwolf nodded – they had talked in depth about Han's past during some of their training sessions.

"When those fuckers decided that they could do whatever they wanted and thought they could get away with it something inside me just snapped. I thought, *like fuck you will*. It's a similar feeling now. The Consortium was created for good, but these corrupt bastards have decided to fuck it all up. Well, I say, like fuck they will."

"And yet, you've gotten away with the systematic murder of close to one thousand individuals," Amwolf said, raising an eyebrow.

"Yeah, I know, I get it. I'm probably the world's biggest hypocrite, but nobody's perfect, eh?"

"I believe that is a safe assumption."

***

Han tried to sleep, but it was futile. He shrugged off his borrowed sleeping bag and left several others sleeping in various corners of the bare bedroom. A floorboard creaked as he reached the door and he felt eyes upon him. He whispered, "Sorry" to no one in particular and crept onto the landing.

After re-dressing his leg, he rummaged through the kitchen cupboards in search of anything that could help pass the night. He eventually fell upon a dusty bottle of vodka. It was a cheap supermarket's own brand, but it would do.

"Pour me one too, while you're at it," Gabriel said, standing in the doorway.

"I was going to neck it from the bottle, but sure, I can be civilised on occasion," Han replied. He located a couple of grubby glasses and filled them up, handing one to Gabriel.

They both took hearty gulps, grimacing at the angry heat.

"It's no eighteen year old Scotch, but it'll do," Gabriel muttered, studying the glass.

"I've tasted better turpentine," Han said then took another sip.

They stood in silence for a time, lost in their own thoughts. Then, cradling his glass, Han leaned against the kitchen worktop and said, "How many of your merry band do you really trust? If any?"

Gabriel drank some more vodka as he contemplated the question. "Three or four."

"Which is it? Three or four?"

"It's either three without you or four with. The jury's out on that."

Han managed a hollow laugh then drained his glass. "I guess I can accept that. Were you expecting me to sneak off in the night?"

Gabriel shrugged. "The thought did cross my mind." Staring at him, he added, "I wouldn't have stopped you, you know."

Han studied him for a moment and then nodded slowly.

"I am glad you're still here though."

"Cheers." Han contemplated the bottom of his empty glass then said, "So, these other three you trust ... I'm guessing they are Amwolf, Maggie and Cloche. Am I right?" A brief nod from Gabriel. "Can you truly trust them?"

"With my life."

"Fair enough." As Han topped up their glasses, he asked, "So, what if we're already compromised?"

"I'm not just considering that as a possibility, but accepting it as a hard fact." Gabriel took another drink.

Han stared at him, glass hovering near his lips. "Erm ... so why the fuck are we still here then?"

Lowering his voice to a whisper, Gabriel said, "We have to go through the motions – show a façade, so as to make them believe that we do not suspect. They are trying to glean as much information from us as possible before eradicating us."

"Eradicate ... that seems so ... absolute," Han muttered.

"Believe me, I do not use the term lightly. Once they get as much as they can from us, they will wipe us off the face of the Earth."

Han finished his glass and poured himself another. "So where the fuck does that leave us?"

"With two plans."

"Ah." The penny dropped. "So, why are you telling *me* this?"

"Because, whether I can trust you or not, I bloody well know for certain that the Consortium can't trust you."

"Good point."

***

At first light, the farmhouse bustled with activity. Teas, coffees and toast were being consumed as bags and equipment were packed into various vehicles. Once everything was loaded and everyone was congregating outside, the farmhouse was then swept top to bottom to remove any trace of their presence.

Han watched from the car as Gabriel said his goodbyes to the rest of the group. It occurred to him that to most of them, Gabriel was saying a final goodbye. Most, if not all of these people were going to die. No doubt about it. Of course, there was a good chance that he was going to die too. Again.

He glanced over his shoulder. Cloche was not watching the proceedings – he had his eyes closed and his lips were moving soundlessly. He opened his mouth to speak, but then thought better of it. He turned back to see Gabriel walking back to the car.

In small groups, the Consortium fifth colonists then headed their separate ways.

As Han, Cloche and Gabriel drove away, Han felt more confused than ever. "So what the Hell is the plan … or plans?"

"The plans will be sent securely to everyone as soon as we're set. We have to leave it to the very last moment before revealing the fake plan to give us the best possible chance of accomplishing the real one."

"So, I'm guessing we be the Alpha team, no?" Cloche asked, his eyes still closed.

"Of course. Along with Amwolf and Maggie. The rest of the group will be carrying out the diversion."

"But you know what that means …" Han said, staring at him.

Gabriel took his eyes off the road for a moment and, his tone even, said, "Yes, I bloody well know. The chances of any of them surviving is next to zero. The majority of those people will be trustworthy and are fighting our cause, but I have no way of working out exactly who, so it's suicide for all of them. I know it, but I'm not happy about it, alright?"

"Okay."

With a sigh, Gabriel turned his attention back to the country lane and said, "We need to pick up some equipment and then be in position and ready to move by tonight."

"And that position is?"

"Dartmouth Castle."

"I'm afraid I'm not up on my castles," Han said.

"I didn't expect you to be. We're lacking in time, so I prepared a dossier on the location for you and Tyrone to do some last minute revision. It's under your seat."

"So you've known about the location for a little longer than you were letting on?" Han said as he pulled out the dossier. He scanned each page, which included photographs and schematics. As he finished with each one, he handed them to Cloche.

"Well, I was hoping for some crumbling ruins in the middle of a field, but I guess I'm just not that lucky," Han said, chewing on his bottom lip. "The two accessible points – road and boat – will be guarded with enough firepower to take out a battalion. They will have sentries all over the ramparts with a clear field of fire as far as the eyes can see. Sheer walls and vicious rock outcrops will make a boat landing and climb near impossible and the landward defences make a frontal assault equally impossible. Are you planning on flying in SAS style?"

"The Consortium takes security very seriously," Gabriel said.

"Where's this bogus meeting supposed to be taking place then?" Cloche asked as he scowled at the pages.

"Colchester Castle."

"I would have taken that one over Dartmouth," Cloche added.

"There's a passageway, accessible from the river under the archway," Gabriel said.

Cloche rummaged through the papers, shaking his head. "I cannot find no mention of it."

"It's there," Gabriel replied.

"Even if it is," Han said, "we still have to approach by boat. But, let's say we do get to the passageway, surely the Consortium will know of its existence too."

"They do and it will be guarded, but it's our best shot."

"Oh, that's just dandy then."

***

Gabriel drove them to a run down industrial estate with a twenty-four hour self-storage facility, which comprised of metal shipping containers of varying sizes.

With Cloche keeping watch, Gabriel unlocked a container the size of a small bedroom then he and Han stepped inside. It was stocked floor to ceiling with boxes of weapons, ammunition, equipment and supplies.

Whistling, Han said, "Is this a Consortium stockpile?"

Opening a crate of M4 carbines, Gabriel said, "No, it would be too risky to attempt a raid on a Consortium stash. This is one of mine."

Han raised his eyebrows. *"One* of yours? I'm impressed."

"Be prepared, my father always used to say."

"Mine said, *grow a spine and kill everyone.*"

Gabriel glanced at him. "You did have a somewhat *unorthodox* upbringing."

After the brief stop, Gabriel drove them to a holiday cottage on the outskirts of Dartmouth on the B3205, overlooking the estuary.

Amwolf and Maggie were waiting for them.

Over a Chinese takeaway, Gabriel walked through the plan with the others. Amwolf would provide a land-based diversion, while Maggie, armed with an L115A3 sniper rifle, would target the sentries. Gabriel, Han and Cloche would form the river-based assault team.

Han poured himself another glass of red wine and knocked half of it back. A bottle of Jack or a good single malt would've gone down far better, but the rouge would have to do. "By your own admission, there's going to be a small army in there. They're highly trained and they"ll be armed to the teeth," Han said, shaking his head.

"Go easy on the wine, guys," Gabriel said to no one specifically. "We've got to be one hundred percent tonight."

Han offered him a tight smile and ate a prawn cracker.

"And don't be forgetting the rapid response team, breda," Cloche added as his eyes studied Han's every movement. He then glanced disapprovingly at Han's half-empty glass as he took a small sip from his own.

Returning to the subject at hand, Gabriel said, "It's nice to know you've both been listening then."

"Given the location and the resources at our disposal, it is the best plan available to us," Amwolf interjected.

"I agree," Maggie added. "With only five of us, it's our best shot."

"I suppose it worked for Richard Burton and Clint Eastwood," Han said as he picked up his wine glass. Hovering at his lips, he reluctantly thought better of it and placed it back down. He ate another prawn cracker instead.

"Now that is a good movie," Cloche said absently. Despite himself, he smiled, but then quickly quelled it.

Amwolf rolled his eyes. "I know the film that you speak of. Of course, one Englishman and one American manage to destroy an entire SS division. American propaganda nonsense."

"If it was American propaganda, Richard Burton would've cocked everything up and Clint would've saved the day." With a wink, Han added, "Zee Nazis didn't stand a chance against Richard's brains and Clint's brawn."

"Well, at least you did not say Germans."

"I'll be assuming the war is still a sensitive issue then?" Cloche asked.

"The compelling tragedy is that there appears to be no desire to learn any lessons from it," Amwolf said.

"Before we get into a deeply philosophical debate about humanity's innate desire to destroy itself, does anyone have any final questions?" Gabriel asked as he began clearing away empty cartons and packaging.

Han slumped into an armchair, shaking his head. Cloche remained silent, staring at his glass. Sitting cross-legged on the rug, Amwolf shook his head. Maggie had been lying next to Amwolf, but now she rose and helped clear away the remains of the takeaway, heading into the kitchen with Gabriel.

Han glanced at Amwolf and cocked his head towards the kitchen.

Amwolf offered a noncommittal shrug by way of answer.

HAN WHITMAN   GABRIEL   TYRONE CLOCHE

WHERE EAGLES DARE

Broadsword calling Danny Boy.

CHAPTER 10

The Zodiac rigid inflatable boat skimmed over the choppy water of the estuary, a grey smear in the darkness. Gabriel steered the quiet, military-grade engine, while Han and Cloche perched at the bow, weapons ready.

First Maggie's, then Amwolf's voice came through their earpieces, confirming that they were both in position.

As they rounded the headland, the bank rose up into black, menacing cliffs.

"Sixty seconds," Gabriel said.

Han switched his M4 carbine from safety to semi-automatic and glanced over to Cloche, who was doing likewise.

They were dressed in black combat fatigues, with balaclavas and night vision goggles. It was a paintballer's wet dream. Despite the fact that he was almost certainly on some fucked up suicide mission, Han was actually having a blast.

It wasn't exactly what he would have envisaged if someone had asked him twelve months ago where he would be, but it was a bit of a boyhood Commando Comic fantasy. Besides, as he had already accepted, he had nothing better to do and no one left in his life, so why the fuck not? This was like being a film extra … in real life … with a cool fucking gun.

Cloche glanced over at Han. "This is gonna be fun!" Han said to him, beaming. The image of Thomas Haden Church rampaging towards a group of golfers, swinging his club over his head, sprung to mind. He burst out laughing.

"Cha, you ain't a full shilling, Whitman."

"It has been said before, mate. If I wasn't a psychotic serial killer, I might start to get a complex."

The castle walls rose up in front of them and then, as they drew close, the rocks appeared to part and they were suddenly travelling under a stone archway.

Gabriel cut the engine and the Zodiac coasted into a subterranean cavern. Sea air mixed with damp rock and the only sound was of the waves gently lapping against the cave walls.

There were sheer walls all around, apart from a short stretch of dock hewn from the bedrock, with a single door leading to the castle's lower level.

A single suppressed gunshot caused Han to snap around just in time to see a dark figure sliding into the inky water from the dock.

"Get your bloody game faces on," Gabriel said, holstering his pistol.

Cursing himself, Han jumped from the boat and covered the door. Cloche and Gabriel followed, Gabriel pausing to tether the boat.

"Remember," Gabriel said, "hard and fast."

Han opened his mouth, but Gabriel cut him off. "Not now, Han. As soon as they realise they're under attack the meeting will be terminated and they will initiate emergency escape protocols. That will give us ten minutes at best. We *have* to get them all before they run."

Without further delay, Gabriel went through the door, keeping low, his suppressed pistol leading the way. Cloche and Han followed as Gabriel opened fire, dropping two suited guards that had been conversing in the stone corridor. He was past them before their bodies had stopped twitching.

154

Both guards had neat bullet holes in their foreheads and blood was pooling in the cracks of the stone floor around them. Han was seeing a whole new side to Gabriel and he was impressed. He always suspected that the man was far more than a glorified pen pusher. The man was a stone cold killer *and* a thoroughly nice guy. What was not to like?

The corridor opened into a small vestibule with a stone spiral staircase leading up to the rest of the castle. Gabriel paused at the foot of the staircase, listening.

There were no shouts or alarms, just the gentle moan of the wind.

He ascended the staircase two steps at a time with Cloche and Han hot on his heels.

Another guard was standing at the top of the stairs. His eyes met Gabriel's and before they could register surprise, Gabriel shot him in the head.

Gabriel shoved past him as the man's body struck the stone wall and slid down it, leaving a bloody stain in its path. Another guard appeared from a dark alcove, pistol in hand and opened fire. Gabriel rolled to one side as Cloche and Han opened fire simultaneously.

Even suppressed, the M4s boomed in the confined space, tearing open the man's shirt and jacket. He fell back against a stone seat in the alcove, but continued firing.

As a round ricocheted off the wall just above his head, Han adjusted his aim above the man's body armour and put a three round burst into his contorted face. The man's head split wide open and chunks of pulped brain spilled onto the ground.

"That's it!" Gabriel snapped as he jumped to his feet. "No more than ten minutes from now. We have to move!"

***

Amwolf checked his watch one final time then held the first round in place at the mouth of the mortar tube. He counted down from ten under his breath and then dropped the high explosive round. There was a thump and the tube jerked back against the base plate.

155

Without pausing, he plucked another HE round out of the ammunition crate and dropped that one into the tube. As he continued to drop rounds into the mortar tube, the first shells began exploding inside the castle walls, sending plumes of smoke and debris into the night sky.

Other than the distant dull thuds, for Amwolf, the night was still quiet and tranquil. Within a minute, he had fired fifteen rounds at the castle. That was his limit.

He set an explosive charge by the rig, grabbed his M4 and headed off at a run towards the castle.

***

Maggie watched the first inbound mortar rounds through her scope then as the first one exploded, she aimed at the first visible guard on the battlements. The sniper rifle kicked hard into her shoulder. A second later a shroud of mist appeared where the man's head had been and his body dropped out of sight.

As chaos swept through the castle, Maggie re-targeted and fired again. Another guard fell.

Maggie had a sudden sense of movement behind her. She rolled onto her back, drawing her pistol at the same time.

A figure rushed out of the bushes as a pistol shot rang out.

***

Han, Cloche and Gabriel moved from room to room, heading for the main banqueting hall.

Cloche unclipped a fragmentation grenade off his webbing and tossed it into the next room. As the grenade clattered across the stone floor, machine gun fire peppered the doorway, spraying stone and wood chippings into Han's face.

The grenade exploded and Han ducked inside, tracking left as Gabriel followed, tracking right. Amidst the smoke and debris, Han caught sight of a figure struggling to his feet near the expansive fireplace. He put a three round burst into his chest and followed up with another burst into the guard's face as he toppled out of sight. He moved on, reloading.

Pistol shots rang out from the other side of the room, causing Gabriel to duck behind a ruined oak sideboard. Han couldn't see the figure through the smoke, but he aimed towards the muzzle flashes and emptied a full magazine into the general area. There was no return fire.

They moved on as he reloaded once more.

Gabriel reached the next door ahead of the others. It blew off its hinges and slammed into him, knocking him to the floor and pinning him beneath it.

Han and Cloche dropped to their knees and opened fire through the doorway. Cloche then advanced as Han continued to cover.

"Gabe, you okay, breda?" Cloche asked as he dragged the heavy door off him.

Gabriel coughed a garbled reply as Cloche hauled him to one side.

Han fired another burst then advanced just as a grenade skittered across the floor towards him.

"Grenade!" Han yelled and scrambled for cover.

Cloche threw himself over Gabriel as it exploded.

Han felt a thump to his chest as he slammed into the wall, gasping for breath. A searing pain in his arm joined the throbbing in his leg from his earlier injury at Cloche's Devonshire fortress. Coughing, he glanced down and saw smoking shrapnel embedded in his body armour. His sleeve was also torn and blood was oozing through the tattered fabric. "Motherfuckers," he mouthed to no one in particular.

Cloche moved over to the door, glancing at Han for a moment only to make sure that he was still in the game.

A guard appeared in the doorway, his MP5 tracking left and right through the gloom. Cloche jammed the barrel of his carbine against the man's temple and pulled the trigger. "How you be liking them dumplings?" he growled as the man toppled to one side, brain matter splattering the floor ahead of him.

"I'm getting a Bruce Willis and Damon Wayans vibe here," Han said and managed a brief laugh.

More gunfire tore through the doorway, causing Cloche to back up before he could respond.

Favouring one leg and clutching his chest, Gabriel joined Cloche and spoke into his mike. "The main banqueting hall is just beyond this ante room. We're running out of time here – we need to punch through these bastards before the response team arrives."

Through gritted teeth, Han said, "Really? You don't say. Shall we invite them out to see if they'll settle this over a game of scrabble?"

"How many grenades have you got? I've got one," Gabriel said, ignoring the quip.

Both Cloche and Han had one each as well.

"Okay, throw them all and then we go in hard."

Fresh gunfire erupted from inside the room as the three grenades were tossed inside. As the multiple blasts rocked the building, the three men rushed inside, guns blazing.

Several guards were already on the ground, one or two still squirming. Two guards returned fire. A round clipped Gabriel's shoulder, but he kept limping towards them, firing. He managed to drop one but then his pistol clicked empty.

At the same time, Han's carbine jammed. Cursing, he ran at the remaining guard as he opened fire. Two rounds zipped past his ears then he slammed into him with the full force of his shoulder. The guard doubled over, dropping his pistol. Han raised the butt of the M4 and brought it down on the man's skull with a sickening crunch.

As Cloche and Gabriel caught up with him, he smashed the carbine against the man's head another couple of times. Spots of crimson spattered his face.

Glancing down at the brains oozing onto the floor, Gabriel said, "I think he's dead, Han."

"Not fucking dead enough," Han snapped back and rammed the butt of the carbine against the man's shattered skull one more time for good measure.

Gabriel let out a strained sigh that was marred with pain then continued on.

Han cleared the breech jam in his carbine as they reached the door to the banqueting hall. They could clearly hear panicked voices shouting and arguing beyond.

Cloche swung the door open and Gabriel and Han rushed in. A pistol shot rang out from the frightened gathering of suited men and women clustered down the far end of the hall. The shot went high and wide.

Cloche followed them in as Gabriel and Han advanced on the crowd. The shooter dropped the pistol and threw his hands in the air.

"How dare you," a barrel-chested man, clutching a cigar in his trembling fist snapped. "How *dare* you!"

"Well, I'm glad they're not going to grovel," Han said with a smile. "That would just irritate the shit out of me."

"These *people* don't grovel," Gabriel said, staring at the assembled group.

A middle-aged blonde woman stepped forward, designer heels clicking on the flagstones. "Do you have any idea what you're doing?"

"Yes, I'm afraid we do, Home Secretary," Gabriel replied with genuine sorrow in his tone.

"*We* ensure that Britain remains strong. *We* are the final defence, God damn you!" She jabbed a manicured finger towards them. "You're destroying everything we've struggled so hard to build."

"That used to be true, Home Secretary, but not anymore. You got greedy and reduced this sacred institution to the lowest form of guns for hire." Gabriel's tone turned angry. "I swore to protect this organisation with my life with only one exception – if the Consortium turned rotten. In that, what I naively thought, inconceivable outcome, I swore that I would give my life to destroy it. Well, here I am."

"Very dramatic," Han said. With a wink, he added, "Sent shivers down my spine."

"Your moral indignation is both laughable and hypocritical, Gabriel," the Home Secretary sneered.

"I don't give a damn what you think." He glanced over his shoulder at Han and Cloche and said, "Kill them all."

"About fucking time," Han said as he opened fire.

Two suited men stepped in front of the Home Secretary as gunfire tore into the crowd. A cacophony of screams and cries jostled with the gunfire for supremacy.

Agonised writhing bodies mingled with the dead on the blood-drenched stone as all three men emptied their weapons into the seething mass.

A gunshot rang out from behind them. Blood and brain matter exploded out of Gabriel's forehead and he dropped to the ground, dead.

Han spun around, returning fire.

Lionheart ducked down at the far end of the lengthy dining table, chuckling, "I say, be careful now, you almost hit me there!"

Han dropped down at the other end of the table as his M4 clicked empty. Cloche sought cover behind a sideboard at the same time. "I don't believe I've had the pleasure," Han said as he slammed a fresh magazine into his carbine. He stole a moment to glance at Gabriel's still form, blood pooling around him from the gaping hole in his head.

Cloche was also staring at his dead friend, his eyes wide with disbelief. Turning back to the newcomer, he yelled, "You son of a bitch!" and opened fired. His carbine clicked empty, so he threw the useless weapon aside and drew his pistol.

"Edward Lionheart, at your service!" Lionheart said and offered a companionable wave.

"Charmed," Han said. A woman moaning behind him caught his attention. He glanced over his shoulder to see that she had been shot in the shoulder and was squirming in a most ungainly fashion. "You're flashing your knickers, love," he said and then shot her in the head.

"We met briefly some time ago … in the cafeteria."

Han remembered, but said, "I don't remember – you mustn't have made much of an impression."

160

"I am a great admirer of your work, Han," Lionheart continued, ignoring the dig. "But, I am afraid your impressive reign of terror must end here."

"*Impressive reign of terror?*" Han scoffed. "Who do you think you are?"

Cloche fired several shots. Lionheart ducked to one side, clicking his tongue. "That was discourteous."

"What you gonna do?" Han asked. "Feed us poodle pie?"

Lionheart laughed. "I knew that you, of all people, would get the subtle reference. It is such a pity that we are not shooting the same … what would you say … script?"

"Oh, I'm guessing we're probably in completely different genres altogether! Me in the gritty crime thriller and you in a rom-com. Judging by the flasher mac, I'd say you were the comedy gay friend for the female romantic lead. You should call yourself Rupert."

One of Lionheart's eyes twitched with an involuntary tic, but otherwise he appeared calm and assured.

"The police, along with a Consortium response team, are already on scene, so I fear that we should conclude our dialogue. What do you think?" Lionheart opened fire once more then cast a small device into the middle of the room. It skittered under the table then suddenly began spinning on the spot and belching out thick black smoke.

Han and Cloche opened fire in unison.

The room quickly filled with smoke and Han then noticed an orange glow within the swirling maelstrom.

Han kept firing until his carbine clicked empty.

Cloche appeared beside him. "We have to be getting out of here."

Above the rising crackle of the fire, they now could hear multiple police and emergency services sirens.

"No shit," Han said. "I say we leg it back to the boat – that bastard's long gone."

"I agree." Cloche glanced over towards Gabriel's body, where it was only just visible through the smoke. His eyes dropped to the floor and then, through a clenched jaw, he said, "Let's go."

A mural was the source of the fire, flames already licking at the ceiling. They ran through a shower of embers into the anteroom. There was no sign of Lionheart.

Han paused and glanced back at the banqueting hall.

"Move it!" Cloche yelled at him.

Reluctantly, Han followed.

Lionheart stepped out of the alcove, a handkerchief covering his nose and mouth against the choking smoke. He walked over to the mass of bodies.

"It is safe now, Ma'am," he said with a glance back towards the door.

The Home Secretary shoved the dead bodyguard off her chest and broke into a coughing fit.

Lionheart helped her to her feet, noting the bullet wound in her arm. "Would you like me to see to that for you?"

"Leave it," she snapped at him. "I want those two traitors dead. You hear me? *Dead!*"

A smile played across Lionheart's quivering lips. "Oh, I think I can come up with something rather special for them." With a nod towards Gabriel's body, he added, "I believed Gabriel to be one of the righteous. Such a pity."

***

As the Zodiac sped away, Han stared back at the castle as it faded into the darkness. Two helicopters were buzzing overhead, disrupting plumes of smoke rising up from several fires still burning within. One continued to circle, its searchlight sweeping over battlements, as the other dropped out of sight behind the fortifications.

A sea fret had settled over the estuary, brought in by the northerly wind. Han felt suddenly alone and isolated.

Gabriel was gone and both Maggie and Amwolf were not answering their hails, so it was probably safe to assume that they were dead too.

162

But, the Troy Consortium's leaders were dead, so their mission had been accomplished. The cost was high indeed, but it was done and that was that.

You're not a bad person, a voice whispered to him. An image of Gabriel slumped in a chair, cradling a glass of whiskey came to mind. He looked tired, troubled. Beaten.

"This shit is over," Han muttered to himself. "Now what?"

"*This* shit may be over," Cloche said as he steered the boat, "but we be still having unfinished business."

"You're not still pissed off about the whole trying to kill you misunderstanding?"

"No, bwoy, I'm pissed off about you murdering Kim." Cloche's eyes locked onto Han's before turning back to the job at hand.

Han continued to stare thoughtfully at Cloche. It would be extremely easy to kill Cloche right here and now. It could even be classed as self-defence. But no, that wouldn't be very sporting of him. Besides, he was actually starting to like the bloke, against all odds.

"If you be going to kill me, just get on with it," Cloche muttered without turning.

Han feigned a wounded expression. "How could you say such a thing after all we've been through together?"

"I *am* still going to kill you," Cloche said.

Han shrugged. "Fair enough. I guess I deserve it and then some. So how do you want to do it? A knife fight all dressed in black?"

"No, I was thinking fists will be just fine. I'll be killing you with my bare hands."

"So am I making you wear the glasses or is it you making me?"

"Say what?"

Han smiled and opened his mouth to retort, but instead, he sighed and said, "Never mind."

Shaking his head, Cloche said, "Cha, you talk more bumbaclut than a politician on polling day."

THE 4TH FILM BY QUENTIN TARANTINO

KILL
THE HOME
SECRETARY

VOLUME 1

WRITTEN AND DIRECTED
BY QUENTIN TARANTINO

Silly rabbit.

CHAPTER 11

It had been agreed that they would wait for one hour at the pre-arranged rendezvous point.

After showering and disposing of their bloodied fatigues, Han cleaned and patched up the shrapnel wound in his arm and re-dressed his leg wound.

They grabbed a bite to eat while they cleaned the cottage and loaded the equipment into the car.

Two hours passed before they reluctantly drove off into the cold misty morning. In that time, neither Amwolf nor Maggie showed up. They were on their own.

Cloche knew of a safe house near Oxford, so they decided to head there. That's where they would settle their unfinished business.

As they drove in silence, Han thought briefly about the clichéd racist gangster and his emo daughter. They were heading the other side of Oxford, but the daughter's anguished face materialised nonetheless.

With the inactivity of the car journey, it did not take long for his thoughts to turn to Cara and their child. He wondered again whether he had a son or a daughter. What had Cara called the little tyke? If it was a boy, he was pretty sure that she would not have called him Hannibal Junior. That would be a safe bet.

The sombre silence was broken only by the drone of the engine. Han slumped deep into his seat, fatigue taking him in its unyielding embrace.

To fight the urge to close his eyes, Han turned on the radio. Chris Rea's, The Road to Hell was playing. Han snorted his amusement and glanced over to Cloche. The man was stone-faced, staring at the motorway stretching out in front of them.

The song finished and a news report followed.

The first report was a breaking news item about coordinated terrorist attacks at Colchester and Dartmouth castles, where low key government select committee discussions had been taking place. Details were still sketchy, but it was understood that there were a number of casualties. It was thought that the attacks were not linked to the Olympic Games. The next item covered last minute security staffing problems for the Games.

Han listened with waning interest until the next item began. In an unrelated incident, the Home Secretary had been rushed to the Royal London Hospital in Whitechapel after a traffic collision in the city. Her injuries were not thought to be life threatening, but she would remain there overnight for observation.

The news item had also grabbed Cloche's attention. "What the hell did he say?" he said, tearing his eyes from the road for a moment to glare at the radio.

Han sat up, weariness rapidly in retreat. "That … nah, it's got to be a bluff to buy some time. Surely." He was having difficulty convincing himself.

Cloche shook his head fiercely. "No, man, if that be the case they would've said that she had been badly injured or something. They would not be saying that she was just being kept in overnight for *observation*."

Han scratched his chin. He sighed and muttered, "Bollocks."

"Is that all you can say?" Cloche growled. "We failed. Gabriel died for nothing, cha bumbaclot!"

"What the fuck is with the bumba-whatever shit? You were educated at Oxford, for fuck's sake. You should speak better Queen's English than me, man!"

Ignoring him, Cloche wrenched at the steering wheel and screamed, "Fuck!"

Opting for sincerity, Han said, "Look, we had to get out of there pretty sharpish – we didn't have time to check pulses."

"You don't fucking say!"

"Okay, calm down, Cloche."

Glaring, Cloche spat, "Don't you be telling me to calm down, psycho-bwoy." He punched the dashboard with enough force to shake the whole car.

Raising his hands in submission, Han said, "Okay, okay. It's a setback, not a total disaster. We can fix this."

"How?"

"Take us to Whitechapel. We'll see where the trail leads us."

Cloche ground his teeth together then muttered, "Alright."

"There is one problem though," Han added.

"What now?"

"Our little fight to the death will have to be put on hold for a bit."

Cloche turned to him. Han offered him an innocent smirk.

***

The journey to London was fraught with delays due to congestion and accidents. The Olympic athletes and their entourages had also been arriving all week in their droves, along with the media circus surrounding them, further hampering traffic into the capital. By the time they reached Canning Town on the A13 both men were stewing in a fractious silence, broken only by a muttered curse here and there.

Han had taken over the driving and was hunched over the wheel, grinding his teeth. There was congestion up north as well of course, but it was minor league in comparison to the Hell on Earth that was driving in and around Greater London.

To add to his irritation, some abortion was trying to force his way into Han's lane by edging the nose of his Audi into his side, expecting Han to bottle it and pull back. Han's knuckles turned white as his grip intensified on the steering wheel.

"Just let the lilly-hose in," Cloche muttered absently.

Han shot him a sideways glance. "I swear to God you're making these bullshit sayings up."

He turned back to the road and maintained speed, keeping parallel with the ill-mannered driver. This seemed to enrage the Audi driver further and he began angrily gesturing and honked his horn repeatedly. When Han completely ignored him, he then swerved in, coming within an inch of Han's car before stamping on the breaks at the last moment.

"Do you speak all Yardie for the sake of your reputation?" Han asked. "I notice sometimes it's more prominent than other times. I bet you speak all posh in real life."

The Audi driver lurched forward again.

Cloche glanced at the fuming driver then turned back to Han. "Why do you speak all American sometimes? Part of your movie persona? Cha, you're originally from Newcastle, you damn hypocrite."

The Audi driver was screaming and gesturing that he was going to do something rather unpleasant. Han let out a sigh and said, "We've all got our roles to play, I suppose." Without another word, he then swerved into the Audi, smashing into its door panel with a grinding crunch. The look of utter disbelief on the driver's face was enough to markedly improve Han's mood immediately.

Cloche slapped his forehead and muttered, "For fuck's sake." He blanked the incensed Audi driver to stare incredulously at Han. "What the hell be the matter with you, bwoy?"

Han offered him a smile and jumped out of the car, heading unhurriedly for the Audi.

After some shoving to open the buckled door, the red-faced Audi driver managed to get out and stood, pointing at the damage. "Look what you've done, you fucking prick! I'm gonna kick fuck out you!"

Han kept walking towards him, smiling. He was feeling much better. It was amazing how quickly his mood could improve, and with such little effort. Out of the corner of his eye, he caught Cloche shaking his head in resignation.

The Audi driver was a rude bully, but he wasn't stupid. Han's unruffled demeanour, easy stride and assured smile started to chip away at his usual arrogance. The brief pause before continuing his verbal assault spoke volumes to Han. "Yeah, keep fucking coming, you cunt," he continued, puffing out his chest. He was a bigger man than Han and clearly pumped his fair share of iron, so although rattled, he was going to make sure that he was the one still standing …

Han's fist came from nowhere and struck the man in the side of the head just on the jaw line. The enraged man was instantly silenced and dropped to the ground like a sack of shit.

He was dazed, but still conscious and was trying to speak through his dislocated jaw. The unintelligible sounds were more Icelandic than Cockney.

The beeping car horns had ceased and dozens of drivers, passengers and pedestrians were watching with interest. Several were pulling out smart phones to start filming. He'd be up on Facebook and YouTube in no time. Would he be seen as the hero or the villain? Did he give a fuck? Hell, no.

In for a penny, he mused and proceeded to kick the ignorant twat in the face until he could see teeth flying in all directions and his face was just a bloody mass. Blood splashed up the side of the white Audi and pooled in the road around the prone man.

Glancing down at the man's caved in face, he thought, *Yeah, maybe the villain …*

Then he walked back to car and drove on without another word.

Cloche stared at him for a while then said, "Feel better now?"

"Much, thanks."

***

They reached the Royal London Hospital half an hour later, but opted to dump the car a few streets away. Cloche picked up a replacement in short order and they transferred their gear into the new one before locating some short-term street parking near the hospital. Cloche reluctantly agreed to stay with the car so that Han could survey the hospital.

With a baseball cap low over his eyes and the collar of his jacket turned up, he headed into the hospital reception. As expected, it was bustling with activity.

After studying the ward list, he opted for Ward 12D, the Trauma Ward as being the best place to start.

On arrival, he explained to the cute eastern European nurse that he was the Home Secretary's cousin. She was very helpful, but it turned out the Home Secretary had been discharged two hours earlier. Bollocks.

"I hope she's not going back to work in her condition!" Han said, fishing.

"No, she's been sent home under strict orders to have at least a couple of day's full bed rest."

"Good – she's a killer workaholic, you know."

***

Han returned to the car. Jumping into the passenger seat, he said, "No joy. She's been discharged – home."

Cloche let out an irritated grunt. "Her home address is secure at the best of times, but she'll be having a lot of extra security now." As an afterthought, he added, "By the way, your little automotive *disagreement* has made the local news, so we best not be hanging about."

"Nice to know I haven't lost my knack."

Cloche rolled his eyes and gunned the engine.

Casting his baseball cap into the back, Han said, "So we have to hit another impenetrable fortress then? I have to say, this is all getting rather tiresome."

The urge to punch him in the face receded quicker than it normally did. Cloche was clearly getting used to annoying psychotic killer quips. Even serial killers can get a bit samey. Who would have thought it? "The quicker we kill her and avenge Gabriel, the quicker we can resolve our unfinished business."

"Absolutely. Breach impenetrable fortress, kill the bitch (sorry, Philip), avenge Gabriel, resolve unfinished business then have a nice cold pint and wait for the whole thing to blow over. How's that for a slice of fried gold?"

Cloche opened his mouth to speak, but then thought better of it and just shook his head instead.

As Han rooted around in the glove compartment for a snack, he added, "So, onward to fortress number two then. Engage."

This time Cloche did speak up. "Just like that then, breda? Not a plan, just a changing of the heading and away we go?"

Han had located a squashed Mars bar and was taking a hearty bite. "Our previous plans haven't worked so well, *breda*, so I say, fuck it. Let's just go down there and cause a ruckus. What do you say?"

"And by ruckus you'll be meaning to kill every motherfucker in the place?"

"Yeah, that about covers it."

"Alright."

***

It took more than an hour to reach the official residence of the Home Secretary in Belgravia. Parking was just as much of a bitch as the travelling.

They donned baseball caps, sunglasses and heavy coats, grabbed two bulging kit bags and headed to the rear service entrance. Before hitting the viewing arc of the door camera, they replaced the caps with balaclavas and both drew combat shotguns. Cloche had already pre-loaded his with several breaching rounds for the door.

Han activated a scrambler, hiding it in the hedgerow near the camera, and then joined Cloche at the door. Cloche aimed at the first hinge and fired. As the door shook he fired at the second hinge, shredding it as easily as the first. Han shoved the door aside and they both moved quickly into a dark utility room.

They carried on through into a kitchen, finding it also empty. As they headed for the next door, it opened ahead of them. Two men armed with pistols rushed in.

Han and Cloche fired as one. Both men dropped to the tiled floor, upper torsos torn and blood-drenched. They stepped over the bodies and headed into a majestic hallway as an alarm began to sound.

"We're on the clock!" Cloche said as he headed for the staircase.

"Like I haven't heard that before," Han replied, hot on his heels.

A guard appeared at the top of the stairs and opened fire.

Cloche pressed himself flat against the plush carpet as rounds zipped overhead.

Han didn't bother to duck. As a round missed his cheek by less than an inch, he returned fire.

The guard flew backwards out of sight.

Cloche was already back on his feet and taking the steps three at a time. Han thundered up the stairs after him, but stopped and spun around in time to see two more guards appear at the bottom. They opened fire.

Han threw himself against the wall, jarring his head and shoulder as bullets peppered the wall, shattering picture frames and showering him with plaster and shards of glass. Ignoring the pain, he returned fire. At the same time, he heard multiple gunshots above him. In the back of his mind, he figured Cloche would not be rushing to his aid any time soon.

The two men ducked for cover. One guard was clipped in the arm, spraying his partner with blood. He fell against the wall, but kept firing. Not bad for a henchman.

Another volley of bullets forced Han against the banister. It cracked against the impact and, for a second, he thought he would crash through it and tumble back down to the floor below. It held, so Han switched the shotgun to fully automatic and squeezed the trigger one more time. The remaining shells were launched in a single rapid volley at the two men.

As the smoke and debris settled, Han quickly reloaded. One of the guards was missing most of his head and the other was gurgling and trying to stop his guts from spilling out onto the floor. He was not succeeding.

Han put the dying guard out of his misery and then started up the stairs. He immediately winced at a sharp pain in his leg. Glancing down, he realised that a bullet had torn into his thigh, not far from the previous leg wound. Luckily it had entered and exited through the flesh, so had not caused any major damage. Still, it was irritating. He rolled his eyes. "Just fucking great. Why me?" He continued with a renewed limp and met Cloche at the top of the stairs.

"What kept you?"

"Good to see you too," Han said as he surveyed his surroundings. He noticed two guards lying dead further along the landing. "No sign of Lionheart yet then?"

"No, but I'm hoping the bastard be at the bitch's bedside."

"Bastard bitches?" Han mused.

"We don't have time for ya bumbaclut," Cloche snapped as he headed along the landing.

They found two bedrooms, a study and a bathroom, all empty. When they reached the next bedroom, they were greeted with a volley of bullets shredding the door.

"Someone's getting a little antsy," Han muttered.

Cloche ignored him. He rammed his fist through one of the shattered door panels and tossed a flashbang into the room. More gunfire followed, but was instantly silenced as the stun grenade exploded.

Han and Cloche dashed into the master bedroom to find a female guard on her knees with her hands covering her face. Han shot her, obliterating both hands and a large proportion of her head. Fingers and brain matter scattered across the shag pile carpet.

Through the smoke, they could see the Home Secretary lying on the bed, moaning.

"Watch yourself, breda," Cloche said, scanning the corners of the lavishly decorated room. "Where is that motherfucker?"

Han kicked open the door to the en-suite bathroom, but found it empty, apart from golden cherubs staring down at him. *That would be somewhat off-putting while dropping the kids off,* he thought absently.

As he rushed back to the main door, he said, "Quite the bordello you have here." He took up a position by the door and peered out into the corridor. No one. Yet.

"No reprieve this time, Madam," Cloche snarled.

Her eyes were streaming and she was clearly disorientated from the blast, but she still managed to say, "This won't change a God damn thing, you idiots."

Glancing over his shoulder, Han said, "Just shoot the bitch."

Cloche did not need telling twice. He squeezed the trigger. The round struck her in the centre of her upturned face, blowing a tennis ball-sized hole through her head where her nose used to be. He put another round into her chest to make sure this time. Blood quickly drenched her satin sheets. "See you in Hell," he muttered.

"Bit clichéd, mate," Han said, but added a wink.

"We can't all be blessed with your finesse."

An explosion out in the street interrupted their banter.

"Armed Response don't normally blow shit up in residential areas, not unless they can help it," Han said.

"Lionheart?"

"Maybe. Let's go."

They rushed back into the corridor and headed back downstairs. As they retraced their footsteps, they found a young female cook hiding in the utility room. She screamed, but they both ran straight past without so much as a glance in her direction.

A police car appeared at the end of the street as they rushed out into the cold early afternoon. Cloche broke into a sprint. Han paused to fire a couple of rounds into the car's grille. The radiator exploded and the bonnet sprung up. It screeched to a juddering halt then quickly reversed back the way that it had just come.

Limping, Han then followed Cloche, shouting, "Shit just got real!"

They drove a mile from the scene before dumping and torching the car on derelict land. They commandeered another and continued out of the city another few miles before repeating the process in a suburban park. They switched one more time, before reaching the countryside. In between, Han patched up his latest leg wound and re-dressed his earlier injuries in irritable silence.

The radio was clogged with the breaking news story of a terrorist attack on an as yet unnamed government minister. There was a lot of speculation of links with the earlier attacks and whether they were specific attempts to disrupt the opening ceremonies of the Olympics Games.

"We made the news again," Han said as he stuffed bloodied rags into a carrier bag for later disposal.

"I'm hoping that will be the last time," Cloche replied. He glanced at Han and added, "You do seem to injure yourself a lot, bwoy. You need to be being a bit more careful, you know?"

Han feigned a laugh. "Oh, you're hilarious. Did you write that?"

Cloche managed a convincing smile and continued to drive in silence.

With his injuries dressed, Han began to feel vaguely normal once more. A thought then occurred to him. He turned to Cloche and said, "We fucking did it, man. Against all the odds, we fucking did it."

"Yeah, bwoy, we did."

"I think Gabe would've been proud of us."

Cloche managed a nod, but remained quiet.

Han opened his mouth to speak, but closed it again. Gabriel had been one of the true good guys, right to the bitter end. It was fair to say that Han had played both sides of the fence on numerous occasions, but not Gabriel. He had stuck to his morals and paid the ultimate price.

We got her, Gabe. For you, mate. Rest easy.

After a while of channel hopping between commercials and inane pop, Han said, "Can we stop and get a bite – I'm fucking starving now. I have been shot and blown up, you know."

With a shrug, Cloche said, "It would be only good manners to make sure I send you to your maker with a full stomach."

Han rolled his eyes. "Ah, yes. I forgot about our prior engagement. There was me thinking that we had a moment back there when we executed the minister."

"You thought wrong."

"Well, I have to admire your persistence," Han said with a wry smile.

"You murdered the woman I loved."

Han shuffled around in his seat to stare at Cloche. "The fucking fucked up Consortium sent me there, man. I very rarely apologise for killing anyone, but I'll make an exception in this case. That was a major fuck up. I'm sorry." Han turned and slumped back in his seat.

It took a moment to register, but then he raised his eyebrows. This was something new. He actually didn't want to fight this guy. Not out of fear of losing, but actually out of fear of winning. He liked him. He hadn't spent this much time with one single person since Cara or Perry. Cara was out of the picture and Perry was cold in the ground. Christ, with everything going on, he hadn't had much chance to think about either of them for a while. The only other new people in his life were either dead or, in Diego's case, sensibly distanced from all this shit. He sat in silence for a time, staring out of the window as the sky slowly darkened.

Cloche had been about to reply, but he caught the distant look in Han's eyes. He watched him out of the corner of his eye for a time. It appeared that there was some small shred of humanity in there after all. Wonders never ceased.

Han switched the radio channel.

"… *will by and by … no true love ways … Sometimes we'll sigh …*"

"You gotta be fucking kidding me!" Han spat and quickly switched channels again. "Why does this shit always happen to me? That's it, after today, I'm never listening to the radio ever again."

Buddy Holly's melancholic tones were replaced with, "*I see a line of cars and they're all painted black …*"

Han let out a sigh of relief and sagged back, closing his eyes.

175

Cloche held his tongue, but continued to observe using his peripheral vision. There was another side to this cold-blooded killer. Hannibal Whitman was a most curious person indeed. He did not trust him one bit, but there was suddenly a vulnerability to the man that he had not seen before. It had slipped through his usual tough and sarcastic exterior in a simple moment of honest regret. He still wanted to kill the bastard, but, damn him, he was making it difficult.

Eventually, Cloche said, "Services two miles ahead. I think they have a Burger King."

You're so sly, but so am I.

CHAPTER 12

Han and Cloche sat in silence eating burgers and French fries amongst the dishevelled business suits, sullen truck drivers and agitated families. The only time they looked up from their food was when two police officers walked in, but they were too busy debating what coffee to order to notice two intense men clocking them.

Shovelling the food in, Han only paused every now and then to rub at his arm or leg. Every inch of his body seemed to take it in turns to vie for attention, each with a gripe of its own.

Han's mobile beeped. With an irritated snort, he pulled it out and opened the waiting text message.

His mouth dropped open mid-chew.

"What is it?" Cloche asked, immediately sensing a problem.

"It's from Lionheart. He's going after Cara." The words all but tumbled out of his slack jaw. Han spat the mouthful of fries onto his tray.

"Who's Cara and how the hell has that psycho got your number?"

Han jumped up from the table, spilling coffee over the half-eaten food. "No idea how that bastard got my number, but Cara's my ex and she has our baby." Amidst the panicking turmoil, somewhere in the back of his mind, he registered the fact that he was now an actual father.

Han was already heading for the door. Cloche followed, while trying to comprehend this new astonishing development. *Han was a father? This man was a fucking father? God help the bully who picked on his child in the playground!* Could he imagine Han dishing out a clip round the ear to an unruly kid? It was more likely that he would force-feed their ears to them.

Han had already started the car and shouted out as Cloche approached at a jog. "Move it or I'll fucking leave you here!"

Before Cloche could close the door Han was already gunning the engine and pulling out of the car park.

Through clenched teeth, Han said, "I'm afraid our fight to the death is going to have to wait … again. That fucking twat has to die first."

"I understand, Han," Cloche said, his tone low and calming. "There are a lot of evil men out there – we are among them, it saddens me to say – but anyone who threatens another man's family is the lowest of them all."

"If he lays one finger on Cara or my baby …"

Cloche struggled to respond, but then simply said, "We will stop him."

As they headed north at over a hundred miles per hour, Cloche asked, "Do we have some sort of plan here? Is there any way we warn her? I'm assuming this lady thinks you is a dead man?"

"Yes and she'd most likely be bitterly disappointed to discover that my demise was somewhat embellished." Han glanced at him then added, "The plan is the same as always – we don't fucking have one, but I do have her number in my phone, if she hasn't changed it again. We could *try* to warn her in some way."

"If we were to keep you out of the equation, she'd think me a sickhead, but if I mentioned you she'd likely think much worse, you know? That doesn't exactly leave us with many options. We could involve the bobs – report suspicious activity or some such."

"Bobs?" Han snapped with an irritated glare.

"Police, man ... Babylon ... Bobs."

Han considered it for a moment then shook his head. "A couple of beat cops would be lambs to the slaughter against the likes of Lionheart. Haven't you watched any horror films? We'd need to drop the fucking SAS on him to give him a bit of a challenge."

"Give me your phone," Cloche said. At Han's quizzical expression, he added, "I'll think of something."

Cloche located Cara's home number and punched it into his own phone. As he read the information that appeared, he dialled the number on Han's phone. A female voice answered after three rings.

"Hello there, madam. My name's Lenny French from the National Grid Incident Support Centre. Am I speaking to the home owner?"

A pause then, "Erm, yes. Is everything okay?" Cara asked.

"We have a report of a gas leak in the area, so we are asking everyone on your street to vacate their homes immediately."

"Is this a joke?" Cara asked, anger giving an edge to her concern.

Frowning, Han mouthed, '*She's a cop!*'

'*I know,*' Cloche mouthed back in return. "I'm afraid it's not, madam. We have notified the authorities and a response team has been despatched to the area. We will be setting up a relief shelter at the community centre ..."

***

Cara had been about to interrupt the man on the phone, but she was stopped in her tracks by a figure stepping into the doorway that led through to the kitchen. That was shock enough, but the man was holding her child.

The phone fell from her hands and she stepped forward. "My baby ..."

179

"Pay attention, Cara," Lionheart said as he tickled the child under the chin. The child did not react in any way, just continuing to stare at him with those brooding auburn eyes. Ignoring the bastard child, he smiled at Cara and continued, "It is absolutely imperative that you follow my instructions to the letter."

Cara stepped forward, her arms outstretched, beseeching. "I don't know who you are or why you're here, but give me back my baby right *now*."

"I will allow you that one shocked response, but your police training should be kicking in by now, so I will not allow you another."

Cara stopped. "Who ... *are* you?"

"You could say that I am an acquaintance of your former lover." Cara opened her mouth to speak, but Lionheart continued, "You were one of the few people who knew his real name. What was it like to fuck a monster?"

It felt like the hallway had suddenly been transported to the middle of a turbulent ocean, pitching violently. Cara thrust a hand against the wall to steady herself as her stomach turned, threatening to empty its contents. "I had ... no idea *what* he was. What do you want?" She held a hand up to her mouth as she gagged. Swallowing hard, she said, "If you're a relative of one of his victims ... I don't know what to say ... I'm sorry for your loss. I'm *really* sorry. At least you can have closure."

Lionheart laughed. "Closure?"

"He's dead."

"Oh, poor deluded child," Lionheart said, his words dripping with mock compassion. "I'm not related to one of his victims and the father of your child is not dead."

Cara shook her head fiercely. "Of course he's dead. He was shot by Carol Belmont and pronounced dead at the scene. I don't know what game you're playing ..."

"This is not a game, Cara. The man known to the world as Hannibal Whitman ... endured. It does not matter how or even why now, but I can assure you that he is very much alive. And on his way here."

"It … it can't be," she muttered weakly as the strength in her legs waned. She did not want to believe the stranger, but somehow something deep inside her knew it to be true. Maybe she had always suspected …

A violent spasm forced her to her knees and she promptly threw up onto the floor, tears streaming down her face.

***

Cloche had heard Cara call out to her baby and then a muffled exchange. He continued to listen with growing dread.

"What the fuck is happening?" Han demanded as his foot pressed harder on the accelerator.

He heard retching and said, "I think–"

A voice interrupted. "Greetings, my treacherous former colleagues. It is good of you to ring and save me the trouble. Do I have the pleasure of speaking to Han or Tyrone?"

"Who? Talk to me, Cloche!" Han yelled and swerved to undertake a Porsche dawdling along at a hundred.

Ignoring Han, Cloche said, "Why be involving innocents in our affairs, Lionheart? We will meet you on your terms – you do not have to coerce us."

"He's there! The fucker's there already!" Han shouted. "You fucking touch a hair on their heads, motherfucker!"

"It sounds like you need to calm your friend down, Tyrone," Lionheart said with a low rumbling chuckle.

Cloche held a hand up to Han, imploring him to calm down. "What do you want?" he asked Lionheart.

"Ah, a pertinent question. I want your heads on spikes. How does that sound?"

"Doesn't sound that good for us."

"A pity, yes."

"Why? The Consortium had gone bad – we had to bring it down. Why you still fighting for them, man?"

Han kept glancing at him, opening his mouth to speak, but jamming it shut again. He seethed, but remained silent.

181

"The Consortium's values and honour remain intact. You are traitors, turned by the Saracen infidels. I will cleanse you from this Earth."

"That's all lies, Lionheart, perpetrated by the Home Secretary and the rest of the Board to trick you into helping them stop us. The Consortium had turned into a bunch of glorified assassins, taking any job from the highest bidder. They were no longer protecting Britain from its enemies."

"Your Saracen lies will not taint me," Lionheart said. "Meet me tonight where Han's journey began. It is only fitting that that is where it should end. If you do not show by midnight, I will slaughter the girl and her bastard offspring." The connection ended before Cloche could reply.

Han glared at him. "Well?"

"We have to meet him where your journey began before midnight or he will kill them both."

Han turned back to the motorway stretching out ahead of them. He let out a deep sigh and his shoulders sank. "Haydon ... of course."

SWEET HOME
HAYDON

Home, sweet home.

CHAPTER 13

It took nearly four fraught hours to reach Shillmoor and Han's anxiety had reached fever pitch. His torment was brought on mainly by his rising distress for Cara and his child, but not exclusively. This would be the first time that Han had returned to Haydon since the massacre.

Given their predicament, it was difficult for him to process his emotions on returning to where it all began. It was the scene of such violence and bloodshed and the beginning of his transformation. As part of that metamorphosis, he had sacrificed many innocents, including several of whom he had genuinely cared for. John Bryce, Big Joe Falkirk and, of course, Lisa and her angelic little daughter, Haley. Would their spirits be still trapped there, waiting for his return? Waiting for their revenge? Could it be possible that Lionheart would be the least of his worries in that … place?

He kept an open mind about that sort of thing and, during darker periods in the past, he had experienced some frighteningly vivid dreams, but he did not truly believe in ghosts or spirits. The harsh reality was most likely that when you die, you're worm food and that's it. But, still, there was always that slim possibility …

In the forefront of his mind, he held on to the desperate urge to rescue Cara and their child to help temper the churning apprehension in his stomach at the thought of visiting his old haunting ground. *Haunting ground?* Not exactly the most appropriate choice of phrase. But that compulsion did help maintain his focus, even though the prospect of standing in Haydon once more still chilled him to the bone.

Shillmoor was a dimly lit spec amidst a sea of darkness that was the rugged Northumberland countryside. Even in the darkness, it was easy to see that it had changed dramatically. There was a café and a gift shop and, if he was not mistaken, a couple more houses.

Han drove straight through without a second glance.

"Haydon is sealed off and there's a twenty-four hour bobs presence," Cloche said as the lights of Shillmoor disappeared behind them.

"I'm sure our friend will have already taken care of any unwanted company." Glancing at Cloche, he added, "And I'm sure he will have been subtle about it."

A gate and gatehouse had been erected at the turnoff to Haydon. A Northumbria Police Land Rover was parked nearby.

Han stopped in front of the gate and they both jumped out. Han opened the door to the small portacabin that acted as the gatehouse and peered inside. The light was on, but the room was unoccupied.

"No one home," Cloche said after checking the Land Rover.

"What a shocker," Han muttered.

After opening the gate, they drove through and headed into Haydon.

As they drew closer, Cloche said, "This man be one of the best, Han. He is strong, intelligent, fearless and utterly relentless. We can't be just rolling up there like a couple of guests late for the bashment."

"You've said that already. But a stealth attack is pointless – he will already know we're here. We don't have time for anything else. And we're not going to be late for no damn *bashment* – we are the God damn bashment!"

"So we just go and serve ourselves up like jerk chicken?"

Han glared at him. "If we have to, yes. Cara and my child are the only innocents in this whole fucking saga, so, I will fall on my fucking sword to save them if I have to."

"That is admirable, man, but if he kills us he will still be killing them too."

Han stamped on the brake, throwing both men forward. "I'm not fucking stupid, Cloche! Some might say that this is my difficult third film. The trilogy is heading for its dramatic climax. I went through the whole *I am your father* bollocks in the second and now I've got to survive the final battle with Emperor fucking Lionheart. I fucking know he'll kill them anyway. I know a twisted psychopath when I see one and I can tell that this bastard is by far the worst I've ever come across – he's more sadistic than I ever was. And believe me, that's fucking saying something."

Cloche shrugged, but then, after a moment's hesitation, he said, "Well, I'm no Lando Calrissian and I'm not being no damn token brother who gets killed off halfway through, so just you remember that, bwoy."

Han stared at him then managed a thin smile. "We better be a whole lot further through this crap than just halfway. I'm beat to shit, dog tired and I'm not as young as I used to be."

"Well, against all odds, we've made it this far."

"It hasn't been through good planning, that's for damn sure."

Cloche stared at him and said, "Does it really matter?"

"I suppose not." Turning back to the road, he muttered, "Well, just so long as he doesn't roll out the Ewoks. Then I'll really fucking lose it."

Han drove on, heading into Haydon with an inevitability that weighed heavy on his shoulders. He was hunched over the steering wheel with grim features.

"We need to work out where and how he's holding them and what tricks he might have up his sleeve," Han said as they drove slowly past the old car lot. It was boarded up, but he could just make out the old faded lettering of *Belmont Cars*. Steve, the Haydon cock's fake 'damn glad to meet ya' smile sprung to mind. Coldplay and broken bottles. *You're a dead man ...*

St. Bartholomew's Church was over the road from the old car lot, silent and dark, like the rest of the village. As if it were yesterday, a vision of the lanky Reverend Dunhealy replaced Steve Belmont, all mess of ginger hair and puffing on a King Edward cigar. *You must be the newcomer I've been hearing whispers about ...* His tombstone teeth glowed like beacons in the darkness, a death head grin welcoming the prodigal son's return.

Han shook the images from his head and continued into the centre of the village. He pulled up at the green, in the shadow of the Haydon Oak.

The village was in shrouded in darkness, pierced only by the car's headlights. A thin veil of mist clung low to the ground, lending an almost ethereal feel to the eerie scene.

Both men sat in the car with the engine idling. They glanced at one another. Cloche's disquiet was a mirror image of Han's.

Han nodded towards the hazy grass on the green. "That's just another piss-take. It really is. What next? Jack the Ripper?"

Reluctantly, Han stepped out of the car. He noticed a police Land Rover parked outside the Post Office, which was still being used as an operations room for the police presence in the village. It appeared as desolate as the rest of the village. After leaning in to switch off the headlights, the darkness became absolute.

The mist displaced with each footstep as Han walked into the middle of the green, dissipating like forgotten dreams. The unkempt grass rustled under foot. It used to be kept so pristine, but now weeds ran rampant and it was dull and limp.

Standing in the centre of Haydon, the silence enveloped him like a silk robe. There was not even a breeze to caress the trees. The mist swallowed up his footsteps and settled around his ankles.

With the stillness, Haydon itself embraced him, welcoming him back to the fold. The SPAR, Merlin's Mea s (still missing the *t*), Little Bakery, Jolly Moe's, The Duck & Bucket and last, but not least, The Miller's Arms. One or two windows had been boarded up, and borders and window boxes had been left to wither and weeds, but otherwise it appeared exactly the same as the night he escaped. The lack of blizzards and drifting snow was the one welcome difference.

He strained to listen beyond the silence, waiting for a solitary howl. Something flickered past the display window in the SPAR. It was barely a shift in the darkness, something just beyond the barren shelves. Then, movement in the upstairs window in the Post Office. A shadow briefly displacing the gloom.

Han felt his pulse quicken as he turned on the spot, scrutinising every dark doorway and crevice.

The curtains fluttered in an upstairs window of The Duck & Bucket. That would be Tess Runckle's bedroom. *So … breaking into my home to peek at me getting undressed …* Smug self-satisfaction oozed from her bloated face.

No, not again, Han thought, his face creasing with dread.

The doorway of The Miller's Arms caught his attention. He turned to catch a shimmer of movement and a faint scraping noise. Then something began emerging from the blackness. Misshapen and ungainly, gradually, a swollen figure shuffled into view …

"Han? Are you alright, man?" Cloche asked, following Han's wide staring eyes to the closed doorway of the coaching inn. "Did you see something?" His hand was hovering inside his jacket where his pistol hung from a shoulder holster.

Han glanced at Cloche's concerned expression and when he turned back, the unearthly apparition was gone and so were the shadows in the other buildings. Shaking his head, he said, "Old memories, that's all."

"I bet."

Han took a deep breath and folded his arms. "He'll be watching us from somewhere." Raising his voice, he called, "Come out, come out, wherever you are!"

"There's that charming subtlety I've come to know so well," Cloche said. "Nice to have you back though – thought I was losing you there for a minute."

A crack like a snapping twig pierced the silence and suddenly Cloche dropped to the ground, clutching his leg. Han spun around on the spot, scrutinizing the darkness for the shooter. He then knelt down beside the stricken man. "Let me see."

In between sucking breaths, Cloche said, "Rifle shot … just above the knee."

"He's wanting you immobilised, not dead."

"Oh, well that'll be alright then!"

Scanning the first floor windows, Han asked, "Did you catch the muzzle flash?"

Cloche shook his head.

"Keep the pressure on. I'll get the first aid kit."

Han ran back to the car and, as he returned with the first aid kit, another suppressed shot split the air. Instinctively, he dropped to the ground and rolled forward, but the shot had not been meant for him.

Cloche tried to muffle his initial cries by wedging his hand into his mouth. The second round had struck him in the same area on his other leg. Blood — black in the darkness — stained the grass around him. He gripped each trembling thigh and repeatedly struck the back of his head against the cold grass.

Han rushed to him, ripping open the contents of the first aid kit.

"Motherfucker ... motherfucker ..." Cloche was muttering through his clenched jaw as his head struck the ground.

As Han patched up the two wounds, he said, "I'm really sorry, mate." His concerned expression validated the sincerity in his words. "I've dragged you into this shit."

"No, Han," Cloche said, shaking his head vehemently. "I was in this shit when that bastard murdered Gabriel ... I was always in this shit."

"You're like me, eh? You just love being in the shit!"

Cloche was sucking in breaths, but his eyes fixed on Han. "Me life as an international drugs and arms smuggler was a walk in the park compared to the last few days with you, my friend." Cloche grimaced then added, "You're a piece of work, Hannibal Whitman. If I live to be one thousand, I will never understand one damn thing about you."

"I'll take that as a compliment, mate," Han said as he finished tying up the two dressings. "You definitely lose some of your Jamaican twang when you're being all serious."

Cloche managed a weak laugh. "Well, like you said, I was educated in Oxford."

188

"Anyone would imagine that I had strolled into some sort of asinine 'buddy' motion picture," Lionheart said as he approached from the direction of The Duck & Bucket. He held a pistol in one hand and had a sniper rifle slung over his shoulder. His other hand was buried in the pocket of his long coat.

Han patted Cloche softly on the arm then stood up and faced him. "So, you decided to finally make an entrance then?"

"It amused me to observe the two of you interacting with one another, but it is time to enter the final chapter."

"I figured you'd be a pervert," Han sneered then, with a nod towards Cloche, added, "That was a cheap shot."

"Sticks and glass houses, Hannibal. Why should you receive any assistance? I do not."

"Fuck you, ya racist battyhole!" Cloche spat.

Lionheart rolled his eyes in an exaggerated gesture of disdain, but a little tic in the corner of one eye betrayed a chink in his cool demeanour. "I am not a racist. I do not care a damn about a man's skin colour or beliefs. I only care when they threaten my way of life. There is a clear distinction between the two."

"Where are they?" Han asked, his thinly veiled patience disintegrating fast.

"They are here in Haydon and they are alive."

"Show me. Right now."

"I am afraid that it is not going to be that simple," Lionheart said, almost apologetic. "I have devised a modest 'treasure hunt' that I am sure you will appreciate. You have thirty minutes starting from …" He glanced down to check his watch. "Now. If you do not find them in time, they die."

"I'm not playing your fucking games, Lionheart." Han drew his pistol and aimed at the man's head. "Take me to them!"

Lionheart shook his head sadly. "I am prepared to die for the cause, but killing me will do you no good whatsoever." He plucked a cigarette box-sized gadget out of his pocket and showed it to Han. His fingers were gripping a spring-loaded lever. "I have no doubt that your Consortium tutors will have instructed you about devices such as this."

Han stared at it and his heart sank. He lowered the pistol.

189

"Very wise, my worthy adversary. If I release the trigger on this dead man's switch your former girlfriend and child will be instantly incinerated."

"You son of a bitch," Han muttered, his eyes dropping to the grass beneath his feet.

Lionheart's tic returned briefly, but he quelled it with a smile that came off as more voracious than encouraging. He said, "I am afraid you are here and you have no choice but to do as I command." Glancing at his watch, he added, "You are wasting valuable time."

Han paused, uncertainty rooting his feet to the spot. He turned to Cloche. "I ..."

"Cha, I'll be just waiting here, if you don't mind," Cloche said and managed a brief smirk. "Now be gone, ya damn fool!"

After a few precious seconds, Han turned and sprinted towards The Millers Arms.

Calling after him, Lionheart added, "I have left one or two surprises along the way for you, just to make the experience a little more ... interesting!"

As Han reached the door, he considered the very real likelihood that The Millers would be far too obvious. But he had to start somewhere and the most obvious place might just be the one a sick fucker like Lionheart would think was the best place to hide them.

"Fuck it." The door was unlocked. He opened it and stepped inside.

A combat knife dropped from above the doorframe and struck his shoulder. Han threw himself to one side, but it was too late. As the knife clattered to the floor, he grabbed at his shoulder where the blade had struck.

His jacket and shoulder were unharmed. Confused, he glanced down at the knife and realised that it was a child's plastic toy. He glanced back to the green at Lionheart who was still watching him.

"Do be careful, my intrepid explorer!" Lionheart shouted, accompanied by a friendly wave.

"Wanker," Han muttered and continued into the pub. The sudden jolt had renewed the pain in his leg and arm. "Oh, the fucking joy," he uttered to the dusty gloom.

Through the inky soup, Han could just make out that his old local was largely unchanged. Everything was covered in dust and there was a scattering of debris on the floor, but other than that it was exactly as he remembered it. There were still racks of glasses, half-filled optics and Big Joe's collection of military memorabilia, including the helmet from his tour in the Falkland's Conflict. *Forty-two years in the Scots Guards ... took that off a dead Argentine captain ...* An acute image sprung to mind, of Big Joe swinging the heavy ashtray like a club and screaming like a deranged William Wallace, *"Bastard!"*

Han's attention was drawn to the floor near the front door. Lisa's blood had of course been cleaned up long ago, but he couldn't help but stare at the spot where the last of her life had ebbed away, a look of utter rage frozen into her features. *I ... loved ... you ...* Surging towards him with hands distorted into claws ...

He had to blink several times to dispel the image.

"Sorry, Lisa." The murmured words escaped his lips without his knowledge, he only seemed to realise afterwards. Uneasy and irritated, he moved on through the bar.

A shadow behind the bar caught his attention, but there was nothing there. Han stood still, staring into the gloom. The silence was pierced by the clink of glasses. He turned to a table near the dust-covered television. A single grubby glass lay unattended, unmoving. It was just an inanimate object, but its very presence seemed to mock him.

My ... angel ... The words appeared to drift on the air.

He spun around, surveying every dark corner. Nothing. Did someone ... *Lisa* ... speak those words or were they just in his head, like so many others?

Gritting his teeth, he said, "It's just your fucking overactive imagination, you dickhead."

He slapped himself hard across the face. As he moved on, he wiped a little trickle of blood from the corner of his mouth with an angry swipe of his sleeve.

He knew that 'Lionstain' prick had left a few boobie traps here and there. The kid's knife had been his twisted little attempt to try to worm his way inside Han's head. *I know your every move*, he was whispering to him. *Fooled you! Next time, it won't be made of plastic …* The next one would be set to maim him. He wouldn't want to kill him, oh no, he would be having far too much fun to let it all end so quickly. No, he would want to toy with him a bit first.

With all that being said, he did not have much time, so he couldn't afford to creep his way carefully around Haydon. He would just have to suck it up. The perverted fucktard would not have had that much time to prepare his little game, so there would hopefully only be a few to contend with.

As he moved through the kitchen, the thought of Lionheart wriggling inside his brain plagued him. Grudgingly, he had to accept that the bastard clearly knew that he would head for the Millers first, setting up his opening prank there.

"He's psyching you out, man," he muttered to himself. "That's my fucking trick."

He continued on, moving quickly from room to room, grumbling to himself the whole time. "Guy's a fucking cliché … if there was a fucking serial killer union there's no way they'd let that knobhead in … Overpriced crusader …"

He kicked each door in and stepped back. It was far from a foolproof plan, but it was all he had time for.

When he reached his old room, he lingered in the doorway. What he remembered to be spacious, light and airy was now dank and oppressive. The pastel shades appeared grey in the poor light and cobwebs hung from the light fitting and corners of the room.

Something caught his attention, partially masked by the foist; the faintest hint of jasmine. He instinctively glanced over to the boarded up window. The bowl of potpourri was still on the windowsill.

We'd just like to ask you a few questions …

Han spun around, shrinking away from the doorway.

The looming forms of Detectives Mitchell and Wright filled the doorway, grinning.

Seems like every time we meet there's a murder …

Click … Wright's red dagger zippo opened and closed … click …

Stove his fucking head in …

Han blinked and was alone once more. He tried to laugh, but it came out as a grunt. To the empty doorway, he said, "Obi-Wan and Yoda, you can just fuck right off."

He had backed up against the bed. Reluctantly, he tore his eyes away from the doorway and glanced down at his old bed. The bedding and mattress had long since been removed, leaving only the wooden frame and slats.

Still, thoughts of a hot late night embrace rushed back. Lisa, naked, breathing hard, clawing at his back, drawing him into her. He felt a stab of arousal, but quelled it instantly with a violent shake of his head. He rushed out of the room, one hand over his mouth to suppress a sob.

After finding nothing in The Millers, he returned to the street and ran towards the SPAR. Lionheart was still on the green with Cloche. He was sipping a hot drink from a plastic cup, the flask down at his feet. The hand holding the dead man's switch was tucked away in his pocket once more.

"You have twenty-five minutes remaining, Hannibal!"

"Would a fucking clue be out of the question?"

Lionheart cocked his head to one side, his expression thoughtful, and then said, "Why not? That would be only sporting of me." After a moment's deliberation, he added, "They are in a building that you frequented on more than one occasion."

Han paused with his hand on the door to the shop. Okay, that was a help. Han had entered most of the houses in Haydon only once to kill their occupants. That left the shops, businesses, pubs, Lisa's flat, the Bryce farm and old Doctor Larry's, if he wasn't mistaken. And possibly the church as well. He entered the grounds twice, but the church only once, but Lionheart might have wrongly assumed that he had attended old Bet Marple's funeral. He had strayed no closer than the front gate on that dreary lunchtime.

He was wasting time. Again.

He opened the door, stepped back then rushed in. Like the pub, it was empty. As he stepped out, he noticed Lionheart was now tucking into a homemade sandwich. Cunt.

Think! he demanded. Where would this prick hide them? The Bryce farm was furthest away and not insignificant. Lisa's flat would be an obvious one, as would Larry's. Too obvious? Maybe, maybe not. Okay, start with the furthest away and work back; the farm first.

Han ran at full pelt for the farm.

"Is this fun for you?" Cloche asked. He had crawled to the oak tree and was sat against it, clutching the tops of his legs. Blood had soaked through his dressings and was dribbling into the grass.

"This is justice, nothing more." With a smile, Lionheart added, "But I must admit, it is rather enjoyable."

"Bully for you."

"One should always find pleasure in one's work."

Cloche couldn't muster the energy to comment further. He shook his head and stared in the direction that Han had headed off in. "Good luck, breda," he muttered, his brow furrowed with a mixture of pain and concern.

***

Han was breathing heavily as he reached the farm. His boots crunched gravel underfoot. The sound fired an image of Lisa into his mind like a lightning bolt, causing him to lurch to a halt, blinking.

Lisa was standing in front of him, fidgeting with flushed cheeks. *I don't do dinner parties ...* He kissed her soft lips. *If they bring out Trivial Pursuit, I'm getting the hell out ...*

Han rubbed his eyes and sweaty forehead then pressed on towards the farmhouse. "I'll ... be right behind you," Han muttered to himself, each syllable catching in his throat like stray fish bones.

Yes, you will.

Resisting the urge to look behind him, he forced himself onward.

The kitchen was empty, as was the study and hallway. He glanced briefly at the door to the under stairs cupboard, where Sally had died, her throat slit from ear to ear.

"Sorry, Sally," he muttered then switched his attention to the floorboards where he had hacked off the collie's head. *The dog's tongue lolling to one side from its lifeless slashed muzzle, a sliver of skin and tissue all that attached it to its torso ... The dog's blood mingling with Sally's.*

Taking several deep breaths, he moved on, stepping around the long gone corpses. He popped his head around the door to the lounge. The two old burgundy Chesterfields were still there, as too were the rest of the Bryce family's furniture. Like the pub and shop, everything was as it had been, apart from the dust and cobwebs. The farmhouse had also had some unwanted guests. Rat droppings littered the floor.

Edging further into the room, Han stared at the sofa where Lisa had sat looking about as comfortable as a vicar in a brothel. He turned to the wall unit that John Bryce had used as his drinks cabinet. The glass doors were opaque with grime, but several bottles and glasses were still laid out on the flip down shelf.

The sound of a cork popping made him spin around. His shin caught the edge of a coffee table and he stumbled onto the sofa, throwing up a cloud of dust around him.

Scrambling quickly to his feet, he caught sight of a figure by the wall unit. It was distorted by the swirling dust, but Han recognised the burly frame.

John Bryce was grinning and raising his glass ... *Here's to a crackin' night ...*

Han fell out of the room and backed against the wall. Coughing, he rasped, "Keep moving." Rubbing at his temple, he turned away to head upstairs. Then he noticed the open doorway to the cellar. The shotgun-blasted door and logs had been stacked against the wall. John had been trapped down there with his dead wife and dismembered son.

The stairs were near pitch black. As with the other buildings so far, the power was off. Han stepped up to the yawning darkness. He opened his mouth to speak, but then closed it again. His heart pounded and he noticed his hand trembling as he steadied himself against the wall.

The thought of descending those stairs into that cellar frightened him more than anything else that he had been through so far this evening.

He took several quick breaths to gather his nerve and then slowly descended into the beckoning void with one hand on the wall for guidance.

A few steps down, Han's foot slipped out from under him. He fell backwards, cracking the back of his head off concrete and sliding down the remaining steps sprawled on his back.

In the darkness at the bottom of the stairs, he groaned and gingerly touched the back of his head. His fingers came away smeared with blood.

His buttocks, back and arms were battered and bruised, but he had managed to escape without a more serious injury. He stood up, wincing with pain. He felt warm blood dribbling down his leg; one of his previous injuries must have reopened with the fall.

He checked the stairs and noted that they had been doused in cooking oil. *Bastard.*

The fall had assisted him in one small way. It had helped focus his senses and pacify his hammering heart. He concentrated on his anger and pain, forcing back his rising fears and paranoia. "It's all good," he said finally. His voice sounded distant and distorted in the oppressive confines.

He stepped back into the cellar, scanning the black depths. Silence and darkness pressed in around him.

He remembered that he had a small LED flashlight. As he patted his pockets searching for it, he heard a faint scrape.

As quick as it was to hearten him, the anger suddenly abandoned him. He stepped back, eyes straining to pierce the inky soup. Another scrape, followed by something dragging across the floor. Frantically, he searched his pockets for the torch. He must have lost it somewhere, God damn it.

Han took another step back, his heel touching the bottom step. There was a shift in the darkness, another scrape then a malformed shape, low to the ground started drawing nearer.

196

"Oh, fuck this shit!" Han scrambled up the steps on his back, his eyes fixed on the foot of the stairs. As he reached the top, he thought he caught a glimpse of a small hand clutching at the bottom step. It looked grey and withered.

Gasping for breath, he backed up until his back struck the shotgun-blasted door leaning against the wall.

It was impossible to keep from admitting to himself that he was unnerved. That was an understatement of gargantuan proportions. He was far beyond unnerved, so much so that if he looked back, he probably wouldn't be able to see it beyond terrified.

He turned and punched the door with enough force to split the panel in two. The previous damage would have helped, but it was enough to send a shooting pain up his arm that radiated out to his other injuries.

He screamed then fell silent once more. The pain and anger had returned, but their hold was tenuous at best. His two faithful companions had also been joined by a healthy dose of irritation. This whole bullshit game was starting to resemble a really bad horror spin off of Home Alone. *Keep the change, ya filthy animal!*

He opened his mind to thoughts of Cara and their baby. They were a welcome, but transitory, distraction.

Conscious of the time that he was wasting, but also desperate to get as far away as possible from the cellar, he made his way back to the kitchen.

Leaning against the sink, he felt drained, aching and suddenly quite ravenous. He touched his matted hair and examined the now tatty and dirty dressings on his leg and arm. The newest dressing on his leg had unravelled and blood had dribbled down into his boot. He was a fucking mess.

Realising that he wasn't going to be any use to anybody in his current state, he stole a few precious seconds to search the cupboards. It revealed plenty of tinned foods that would still be edible. He opened a tin of tuna and greedily forked the contents into his mouth before continuing into the night at a limping jog.

He had less than ten minutes remaining when he reached Doc Larry's house. He pushed the door open. As he stepped back, he heard a click. An explosion followed. Han threw himself to one

197

side as buckshot peppered the opening, several striking his leg and one nicking his side.

Lying in the gathered muck, clutching at his stinging leg and side, he screamed, "Son of mother fucking whore!"

A quick examination revealed that the pellet in his side was just below the surface, so he dug it out with his fingertip, grimacing at the heightened pain. He should have put his body armour back on, but everything had been a bit of a blur since rushing out of the Burger King several hours earlier.

The other three pellets in his already injured leg were deeper, so he left those in place and stood up.

Hobbling inside, he noticed a double-barrelled shotgun had been hooked up to a simple wire rig. When the door opened far enough it exerted sufficient pressure to depress the triggers.

"You cheeky mother ..." He let his voice trail off, lacking the energy to bother cursing any further.

Han kicked the shotgun aside and headed into the lounge.

The site of the dramatic climax of the Haydon massacre was untouched. The only difference to everywhere else was that there were still visible SOCO markings on the floor and walls, indicating bullet holes, casings and discarded weapons. Sam and Jimmy's final resting places were also still visible under the dust and detritus.

Jimmy had started off as a snivelling bottom dweller, but by the end, he had experienced something of a renaissance. Now that was real character growth! You couldn't write that shit. Han had mixed feelings about it, though. On the one hand, he felt almost proud to have dragged him out of his drug-fuelled lethargy, but on the other ...

He didn't have the time to dwell on any of that historical bollocks right now. He had to find Cara and the baby and he was running out of time.

Something caught his eye, something that looked out of place. There was a picture frame on the mantelpiece that did not have any dust on it. It had been placed there very recently. It looked like one of those tacky embroidered religious messages that someone's granny might have knitted. It said simply, GOD IS WAITING FOR YOU.

"Fucker."

Han ran from the house, ignoring the pain in his leg and the chorus of protests from the rest of his battered body. He cut through the back lanes to shave off a precious minute as the clock counted down inexorably to the dying seconds.

With no time to linger, Han flung the doors open to St. Bart's and, gasping for breath, staggered inside. The agony in his bleeding leg finally overcame him and forced him to his knees just inside the doorway.

He was covered in blood, grime and sweat and bore an uncanny likeness to how he looked by the end of his previous visit to Haydon.

That's it, man, game over.

CHAPTER 14

As Han coughed and gasped on his hands and knees, he was greeted with a slow clapping from further inside the church. Lionheart was standing in front of the altar, smiling.

Between gasps, Han said, "I've only been in here once before, you prick."

Lionheart feigned apologetic surprise and said, "My humble apologies."

It was then that Han began to take in the rest of the scene behind Lionheart. Cara was strapped to a ten foot roughly hewn cross. He remembered the church only having a simple brass cross the size of a standard lamp, so it was clearly a Lionheart addition. She was semi-conscious, her head lolling and staring wildly.

Cloche was similarly secured across the pipe organ, hanging by his tethered arms. Blood was pooling around the base. He was alive, but out of it, most likely due to blood loss.

Finally, there was what looked like a little bundle of rags resting precariously on the edge of the font. But then it moved.

"This is clichéd even for you," Han said, glancing back and forth between Cara and the child. Groaning, he struggled to his feet, wincing with every minute movement.

His air of self-satisfaction wavered briefly with the tic resurfacing. It was gone in an instant, but not without Han taking note first.

"What you describe as clichéd, I would call classic," Lionheart replied with an overemphasised sweeping gesture around him.

"Is that … *you?*" Cara said, her eyes settling on Han. Her brow furrowed as she tried to focus. "Could it be?"

Han managed a brief wave with one hand before it dropped back down to his side. "Hi, hun."

Cara's mouth dropped open, seemingly working soundlessly for a time. She was clearly still somewhat dazed, but she managed to say, "Hi, hun? … Wha? Hi, *hun?*" She licked her dry lips and swallowed to lubricate her throat then managed to fully focus on him. "He … he said you were alive, but I couldn't believe him, not without seeing you with my own eyes." Tears welled up in her eyes and she choked back a sob. "You look … different, but it *is* you. I know it."

Han struggled to find the words, but could only manage a lame, "Sorry."

"Sorry?" A single tear fell to the stone floor at her feet. "You murdered hundreds of innocent people … even … *kids.*" The last word fell from her quivering lips like a retch. Her attention turned to the font. "My baby! *Our* baby!"

"As touching as this reunion is," Lionheart said, "I'm afraid I am going to have to interrupt as we are on a rather tight schedule."

Han slowly stepped closer to the altar. "You win, Lionheart – I'm here. You've got both of us, so you don't need them anymore. Let them go."

Lionheart emitted a short laugh and shook his head. "Hannibal, Hannibal, you are not naïve enough to believe that it would be that straightforward."

"I thought you were supposed to be a man of integrity."

"My integrity is without question. I instructed you to make it here within thirty minutes or they would die. I mentioned nothing of the next stage once you had arrived."

His anger partially refuelling his spent reserves, Han said, "Let them go, you twisted little fuck. They're innocent – they have nothing to do with any of this!"

Lionheart's tic returned. "They have everything to do with this." Jabbing a finger at Cara, he added, "That whore lay with the enemy and that creature is the bastard offspring."

"You're starting to look a little unglued there, mate," Han said, lowering his tone. "It must be hard being cast adrift, the Consortium gone, your pathetic crusade lost."

"The cause is not lost!" Lionheart bellowed, the tic in his eye going into overload. Glaring at Han, added, "The war will continue with or without the Troy Consortium. And I *will* ensure victory!"

"No need to be so tetchy."

Lionheart drew in a deep breath and the tic gradually subsided. Regulating his tone once more, he said, "Let us *crack on*, as you would say."

Han managed a humourless laugh and said, "Okay, dickhead, now what?"

"I am delighted you asked." As Lionheart walked over to the font, he produced a remote control from his pocket. Han at first mistook it for the dead man's switch, but this was something else.

"More gadgets up your sleeve?" Han said. He folded his arms and stepped closer. Both gestures resulted in shooting pains in various parts of his body, but he managed to conceal them well enough.

"You are going to love this."

"I kinda doubt that."

Lionheart pressed the button.

With a series of clicks, the cross slowly started to rise off the ground and pitch forward.

Cara suppressed a gasp. Ignoring her own predicament, her eyes fixed on Lionheart as he reached her child. Any remaining confusion evaporated. "Whatever this bastard wants, give it to him!" she screamed at Han. "Whatever his twisted plan is, SAVE

202

OUR DAUGHTER!" Her eyes burned into Han's with an intensity to rival Lisa's. "Fuck you and fuck me too! My baby girl is all that matters! Do you hear me, God damn you?"

Han edged closer, but he stared back at Cara as she was lifted further into the air and pivoting to face the stone floor. "I hear you, Cara. Whatever it takes." Somewhere in the back of his mind, it registered that his child was a girl. He had a daughter.

At the font, Lionheart scooped up the child. As he did, with his other hand he pocketed the remote control and withdrew a pistol.

Stepping closer, Han noticed smoke belching from the back of the pipe organ.

It was pretty obvious where this was heading. He still had his own pistol, with which he could try to shoot Lionheart, grab the baby and then try to save Cara by recovering that remote control. Cloche would have to be last. Flames were already licking up the pipes. He didn't have long. Clearly none of them did, that was the whole point. He could try to save one at best and that had to be the child.

The time for thinking was over. He ran towards the font just as Lionheart dropped the child into the water and pressed her down beneath the surface. At the same time, he aimed the pistol and fired.

Han was too concerned with closing the distance between them to attempt to evade. The bullet struck Han in the thigh, sending him sprawling into one of the pews. The bastard had picked his shot well, choosing his relatively uninjured leg. He hit the solid pews hard, splitting his head open and coming to rest in an agonized twisted heap.

Cara was screaming hysterically, wrenching and twisting against her bonds. "My baby!" The cross was still climbing, nearing the rafters.

Han was already scrambling to his feet and surging towards the font once more, leaving a smeared bloody trail in his wake. He swept streaming blood out of his eyes as he ran.

The crack of a gunshot barely registered as he stumbled forward, but he saw Lionheart twitch and stagger back away from the font, a spray of blood erupting from his neck.

Han fell against the font and plucked the squirming child out of the water. He spun around to see Amwolf rushing down the aisle, carbine in hand.

With Han's attention briefly diverted, it was all Lionheart needed. With one hand pressed against his bleeding neck, he levelled the pistol at Han and fired. Han was turning back as the bullet sliced a groove into his forehead, crisscrossing the earlier gash from the pew. Fresh blood gushed down his face.

Han was blocking a second shot at Lionheart, so Amwolf yelled, "Throw her!" as he sprinted to close the gap.

Han had no time to consider the consequences. He threw the tiny bundle towards Amwolf then turned and launched himself at Lionheart.

Lionheart was taking aim to fire again, but instead he cast the pistol aside and surged forward to meet him, bloody hands outstretched like talons. They collided like the impact of two planets, both men snarling and grunting and blood spraying in all directions.

Badly injured and exhausted, all of Han's training deserted him and what ensued was a bloody brawl of fists, teeth and limbs. Nails tore at Han's face as they crashed into the burning pipe organ. Somewhere at the back of his mind, Han hoped that Amwolf was somehow saving Cara and Cloche, but there was nothing he could do to help.

Han managed to slip an upper cut in between Lionheart's scratching hands that knocked the man back a couple of steps. He instantly returned for more, gouging his fingers into the gashes on Han's forehead, tearing a flap of skin loose. His face loomed close and his teeth snapped at Han's nose, ripping into the delicate flesh at the tip.

Han fought to keep this wild animal off him, shoving hard and then following up with several jabs to the face. Lionheart was like no other person he had ever fought before. This was no man.

Blood and spittle flying from his contorted lips, Lionheart screamed, "You sided with *them* – the enemy! You traitor!"

"You don't know what the fuck you're talking about," Han managed as he parried two more blows. He caught the side of the man's head with the blade of his hand, but it failed to slow him down even for a second.

"You have no idea what they've done! What they're capable of!" Lionheart's rage rose to a whole new level and he flung himself at Han once more, scratching, biting and snarling.

The brutal onslaught forced Han back against the font, jarring the small of his back against stone. Still Lionheart lashed at him.

Several gunshots rang out and Cara's screams heightened to one long shriek. The cross suddenly swung violently as the pulley gave away with Amwolf's shots. As it swung vertical, a small explosive charge in the rafters ignited and the whole thing came crashing down.

Han caught sight of Amwolf rushing forward as the cross toppled over onto him. Then more nails and teeth engulfed him, forcing him over the font, back screaming in agony.

The crackling fire from the pipe organ began to singe Han's head and the intense heat scorched the back of his neck. He could only hope that Amwolf had either dragged Cloche to safety or that he had remained unconscious while he was barbequed alive.

Foaming spittle struck his face like hot lava as Lionheart screamed, "I will slice you into a million pieces and feed you to the rats!"

Lionheart's red cross dagger appeared inches from his face. Han managed to yank a hand free from the weight pressing against him and grabbed at the blade as it was thrust against his face. He felt his palm rip open as the blade sunk into his flesh. He howled in renewed agony, but it was enough to arrest the blade's momentum and reward him with precious seconds. Blood splashed into his already smeared face.

"Fucking choke on it!" Han cried and rammed his forehead against the bridge of Lionheart's nose. The crack was audible even above the roaring fire. Lionheart staggered back, shock marring his fury. Han moved with him, his hand still firmly clamped around the blade.

As he fell back into range, Han head-butted him again and again, splattering blood across the floor around them. Both men were awash head to foot in each other's blood.

Thick smoke swirled around them but still they fought on.

Lionheart coughed blood into Han's face, baring red teeth. Blood was gushing from his pulped nose and the gunshot wound in his neck.

Han thrust his fist into the man's nose one more time, feeling cartilage pop and click.

Lionheart's head snapped back. As he stumbled backwards, his legs failed him and he collapsed to his knees, the dagger falling from his hand.

Han threw himself onto the gasping man, his own teeth now his best weapon. He took a chunk out of Lionheart's cheek as the man screamed with frustration. As he continued to thrash Han dropped lower and snapped at his neck. The bullet wound was only a nick, but his neck was soaked in blood, making it slick and awkward to grasp.

Lionheart lashed out once more, a blow connecting with Han's kidneys then nails raking the side of his face.

Han grappled with him and they both fell to the floor. Still Lionheart squirmed and fought beneath his weight, fists, fingers, knees all striking him from different directions. With his second attempt, Han's jaws locked onto the man's jugular.

Lionheart's mouth stretched impossibly wide. "Not right!" he shrieked in disbelief.

As his teeth sank into greasy flesh, Lionheart managed a gurgled "No!" then Han wrenched his head to one side, ripping open the man's throat.

The man pulled the covers from the trembling boy. "You thought no one would catch you in your dirty little sin, boy?" the man said, gripping the boy's slender chin in his unyielding hand and pulling his wide-eyed face close.

"Father, please … I'm sorry."

"Sorry?" the man spat in the child's face, causing him to cower back against his pillow, tears in his eyes. "You lust for the flesh of man? And you

say sorry? It is forbidden! The Quran forbids it and Allah forbids it." He paused, *lips moving soundlessly for a moment as he recalled a relevant verse. "For ye practice your lusts on men in preference to women: ye are indeed a people transgressing beyond bounds.' Beyond bounds!"* he screamed. *"You disgust me, boy."*

"It'll never happen again! I promise!"

"You're right it will never happen again, boy. When a man mounts another man, the throne of God shakes'! 'Kill the one that is doing it and also kill the one that it is being done to', it tells us." As he ripped the pyjamas from the crying boy's body, he said, *"I will not kill my offspring, but I will teach you a lesson you will never forget ..."*

Blood bubbled on his lips and a single word escaped before the man died. *"Father ..."*

The word caused Han a moment of pause, confusion stamped into his gore-splattered face. It only held for a second and then he spat the chunk of flesh into the dead man's wide staring eyes.

He staggered to his feet, staring wildly around the smoke-filled church, coughing and retching.

His head was spinning from blood loss and smoke inhalation, but in a hoarse cough, he managed to cry out, "Amwolf? Cara?"

He caught sight of Amwolf heaving the cross to one side and blundered over towards him. His former tutor was bloodied and injured, but had managed to arrest the fall of the cross and was helping Cara out from under it. She too was battered and bruised, but alive.

Seeing that they were both all right, Han turned and stared at the blazing fire that used to be the pipe organ. Torrents of flames were licking at the rafters and the fire had already spread to the front row of pews. Then his eyes fell upon a figure lying several feet away in the aisle, the small bundle that was his daughter lying next to him.

"He is alright, my friend," Amwolf said between laboured breaths. "We need to get everyone out of here before the entire church is razed to the ground."

Cara and daughter were both crying as they staggered out of the church into the cold night air. Han and Amwolf followed, dragging an unconscious Cloche. Each step was agony and they stumbled every yard. By the time they collapsed near the gate, thick smoke could be seen rising into the sky. St. Bartholomew's modest stone steeple was lost amidst the black maelstrom.

As Han and Amwolf lay gasping and bleeding on the grass, Cara tentatively stepped over to them, her blackened face a mask of conflicting emotions. She clutched the now whimpering child close to her chest, ignoring the trickle of blood running down her forehead from a gash in her hairline.

Han looked himself up and down, squinting through blood-encrusted eyes. He was drenched head to foot, in both Lionheart's blood and his own. He could have doubled for Carrie's long lost brother. Even with his nose blocked with blood and soot, he could still smell smoke.

As he filled his lungs with the delicious fresh air, the faintness threatening to consume him gradually subsided. He had lost a great deal of blood, but he managed to look up from his child to Cara and offer a genuine smile of contentment. With blood oozing down his face and smearing his teeth, it probably looked more like the wild grimace of a lunatic, but it was all he could muster.

"Thank you for saving our daughter," Cara said, her voice sounding impossibly frail in the quiet night. She wiped blood and grim from her forehead with the back of her hand as she seemed to struggle with her feelings for a time. With a sigh that had profound sadness clinging to it, she said, "It doesn't change what you are or what you've done, but thank you."

Han tucked his injured hand into his armpit and gingerly tried to wipe some of the blood from his face with the other. It was futile. He could not begin to formulate his thoughts or emotions into words, so he just managed a nod.

"You cannot ever be a part of our lives again, but you can at least know that Holly will grow up and have a good and happy life with me." Blood dripped down her nose and onto her lip. She swiped it aside and hugged her baby once more. Holly emitted a soft gurgle, recent traumas already receding into distant memory for her.

"I'm sorry, I—"

"Don't," Cara said. "Save it." With that, she turned and walked away, heading for the gate. She walked with a limp and was bruised, bloody and grimy, but there was an unquestionable elegance and fortitude in her demeanour.

You had the grace to hold yourself,
While those around you crawled.
'Candle In The Wind' by Elton John

Han opened his mouth to call after her, but Amwolf placed a hand on his shoulder and said, "No, Han. Let them go."

With a groan, Amwolf pushed himself to his feet and limped over to Cloche. He bent down and checked his pulse then said, "You are both in need of immediate medical attention and we need to get far away from this ... *place*."

Han stared at him for a moment and then, grimacing and groaning, he hauled himself to his feet. He bent over, clasping his bleeding hand between his legs. Looking up at his former tutor, he asked, "Where were you? What happened?"

Amwolf did not answer at first. He gestured for Han to help him with Cloche. With great effort, Han shuffled over, each deliberate step agony.

As they carried Cloche back to the car, Amwolf finally said, "I narrowly escaped Dartmouth Castle. I am afraid Maggie was not so lucky. I failed to make the rendezvous, so I have been playing catching up ever since."

"That's catch ..." Han sighed and said, "Oh, never mind."

Amwolf was too busy concentrating all of his remaining strength on the job at hand to bother with Han's interruption. Instead, he continued, saying, "It then occurred to me that they could use your former girlfriend to get to you. I was too late to stop her abduction, but I was able to follow them here. I could not risk attempting to re-establish communications, so I waited for the most opportune time to strike."

Han was wheezing and waves of pain were washing over him, but he managed to say, "Well ... you saved the fucking day, mate."

209

"Luck more than sound judgement, but thank you."

They stopped to watch Cara drive past in what must have been Lionheart's car. Her eyes met Han's for an instant and then she turned away and was gone.

"I've got a baby girl called Holly," Han said and smiled as he watched the rear lights disappear into the night.

"You are truly blessed, my friend."

As they drove away from Haydon, Han took a moment away from dressing both his and Cloche's wounds to glance back at the dead village. He thought he caught sight of a single slim figure standing on the green, watching them leave. It must have just been a trick of the shadows cast by the Haydon Oak.

Amwolf watched him in the rear view mirror. As he turned back to continue with the first aid, Amwolf said, "So, my friend, have you finally lain the ghosts of Haydon to rest?"

Han looked back as the burning steeple of St Barts disappeared into the darkness. Turning to Amwolf, his expression thoughtful, he said, "Yes, I think I have."

The sun endures. The moon endures. Life endures.

EPILOGUE

Han limped into the coffee shop. His many wounds were beginning to heal, thanks to Amwolf's medical connections, but he still felt like he had gone twelve rounds with Mike Tyson. His forehead was taped up and the tip of his nose had scabbed over.

He caught sight of Tyrone Cloche, sitting at a corner table, tucked away from the other patrons. He offered him a wave of his bandaged hand as he ordered a coffee.

Her expression concerned, the young barista said, "Looks like you had a bad day."

Han snorted. "Yeah, something like that."

Sitting down opposite Cloche, Han said, "You're looking a lot better."

"A lot better than near dead? So I'm still looking like fuckery then?" He glanced at the crutches leaning against the wall and then tentatively touched the back of his head that was still taped, covering up first-degree burns.

Han smiled. "I was trying to be polite, but yeah, you've looked better." With a chuckle, he added, "And you still smell like burnt toast."

"And you look like a bucket of shit, bwoy," Cloche retorted, but then laughed.

The barista brought Han's coffee over and said, "Great news about our medal count, isn't it? Third, can you believe it?"

Han offered her a warm smile. She was pretty, in a petite bookish way. "Certainly is, hun." He caught her glancing back in his direction. It should have pleased him to receive some female attention, but instead it cast a cloud over his mood. He sipped his coffee in silence for a time. He tried to picture the pretty Welsh student, Danielle, to take his mind off the inevitable.

Cloche watched him with interest and then leaned on his elbows and said, "Amwolf has confirmed that the last elements of the Consortium have either disappeared or disbanded."

Han silently thanked him for changing the subject. "So, Gabriel's crazy plan did work then." He thought back to that first day in the hospital room when Mr Average had walked in and flung his raincoat over the chair. So much water under the bridge since then. "He was a good bloke," he said after a time.

"He was," Cloche agreed. "An honourable and decent man."

They fell silent once more, each with his own memories of the man.

It was Cloche who broke the silence. Pulling out an A4 envelope from under the table, he said, "He was also a practical man who planned ahead."

Han set his coffee aside and leaned back in his chair. "Oh yes? What's that?"

Tapping the envelope, Cloche said, "He left this in a safety deposit box for us. It contains keys and addresses of his safe houses and equipment stashes, bank accounts, contacts. Everything."

Han's eyes widened. "You've gotta be shitting me."

"I shit you not, breda."

Whistling, Han said, "Well, that is a turn up for the books."

Still tapping the envelope, Cloche said, "So you still planning on making a go of the writing?"

Staring at the envelope, Han said, "Well, the ghost writer did a bunk, so the job is there for me to slip in to if I want. It might be nice to have a *normal* day job, regardless of what happens next."

"I suppose every superhero has to have their alter ego."

"The jury's still out on that one – they can't decide between hero or villain yet." Cocking his head, Han asked, "What about you? Are you going back into the criminal underworld?"

"Nah, man, I'm done with that facade." Slipping the envelope back out of sight, Cloche said, "So what now?"

Han sighed then looked up from his coffee. "I suppose we've still got that unfinished business."

"I don't think we're in much shape to do anything about it," Cloche said and took a sip of coffee. "Not at the moment, anyhow."

It was Han's turn to laugh. "That must make me MacReady and you Childs then."

"If you say so, breda."

The old wannabe Tarantino, Perry, sprung to mind and Han felt a stab of grief. He would have picked up on the reference. He always got a film reference. He supposed he could educate Cloche in the ways of the film, given time.

"So what do we do if we're not going to kill each other just yet?"

"I think we deserve some time off."

"And then what?"

Cloche shrugged. "Then maybe we just see what happens, eh?

Han mulled that over then nodded. "Sure, we can do that." With a wink, he added, "Partner."

"Don't be getting ahead of yourself, bwoy," Cloche said, smiling. "I still want to kill you … most of the time."

"I do tend to have that effect on people." As an afterthought, Han added, "Fuck it, let's go for a pint and forget the whole damn thing, eh? I'll introduce you to Diego, a mate of mine. I think you two will get along just fine."

Friday night they'll be dressed to kill,
Down at Dino's bar and grill,
The drink will flow and blood will spill,
If the boys want to fight, you'd better let them ...
'The Boys Are Back in Town' by Thin Lizzy

THE END

BIOGRAPHY

Rod lives in the beautiful North East of England with wife,
Vanessa and he's not as mad as his writing suggests …

CHAPTER ARTWORK WAS ADAPTED FROM THESE POSTERS